Redeeming the Night

Kristine Overbrook

CRIMSON
ROMANCE

F+W Media, Inc.

Published by
Crimson Romance
an imprint of F+W Media, Inc.
10151 Carver Road, Suite 200
Blue Ash, OH 45242. U.S.A.
www.crimsonromance.com

ISBN 10: 1-4405-9349-3
ISBN 13: 978-1-4405-9349-9
eISBN 10: 1-4405-9350-7
eISBN 13: 978-1-4405-9350-5

Cover art © iStockphoto.com/grahambedingfield; iStockphoto.com/Chris Pritchard; iStockphoto.com/Yuri_Arcurs.

Acknowledgments

Thank you
    to my family, for your encouragement and support.
    to Laura, my dear friend and butt-kicker.
    to Tara G., your excitement is contagious.
    finally, to Jess V., Annie C., and Julie S., your assistance and insight on this book has helped me become a better writer.

Chapter 1

Smoke rose from torches around the chamber and snaked up the stone walls. The dark cloud pooled against the ceiling before it slipped through the vents. In the flickering light Ashley could easily make out the robed features of the sisterhood, somber in preparation for the coming ritual. The women had welcomed her, supported her, and had given her purpose during the worst part of her life. She owed them everything.

That was forty years ago. *So long?* Decades passed easily in the sisterhood. Those who wore the black onyx band of membership didn't age. As the Mother had slipped the band on Ashley's finger all those years ago she'd said she only welcomed the worthy. Even now, Ashley thanked the gods she had been chosen.

Ashley and the other women began to sway. The ritual had begun. Gold embroidery around the hems of their maroon, satin robes glinted in the torchlight. The Mother stood at the center of the chamber, flanked by two women. Thirteen others, including Ashley, formed a circle around them. Their murmuring chant echoed off the stone, the reverberation adding a deep, harmonious counterpoint, as if the chamber chanted with them.

The women's onyx rings began to glow. Warmth grew and spread through their bodies. They moved in unison, circling, their steps keeping time with the chant.

Pressure built, rising within them. It flowed through their bodies. Coursed over their skin. Their breasts.

Every nerve ignited. They extended their arms toward the center.

The Mother reached her arms upward and cried out something unintelligible. The awakening began. The sisterhood cried out as waves of release shook them. Their bodies tingled and throbbed.

The souls of the dregs of society, harvested for the betterment of womankind, pulsed from them, leaving behind nothing except oneness and satisfaction.

Slowly, Ashley's mind cleared from the shared orgasmic fog.

"Ah, ladies, the harvest of this month was plentiful and your offering bountiful," the Mother declared, extending her arms wide as if embracing the entire room.

Ashley nodded along with her sisters. This was the standard statement following the ritual.

The Mother raised a finger and continued, "So much so, it is time for us to move another to the inner circle."

This brought murmuring. The inner circle currently held two sisters: Lena and Ashley's own mentor, Tarma. Those in the inner circle were the honored teachers. They were the closest to the Mother, and they often took part in private rituals with her. Although the outer circle knew nothing of the rites, they all wished to participate.

The Mother reached a hand toward Ashley. "Sister, you have shown dedication to our course and unity of spirit with your sisters. I will bestow this honor upon you." Ashley stepped forward and placed her hand in the Mother's. Her heart sang. She'd done everything she could to garner praise from those in the inner circle. Now her focus had been rewarded. The Mother's thin fingers belied the strength with which she grasped Ashley's hand. "There are two tasks you must complete before you can take your place."

"Anything," Ashley whispered. The sisterhood had saved her when she'd been used and discarded by the man she'd trusted. With their help, she had spent years making sure other women wouldn't have the same struggles.

"The first task will begin tonight." The Mother nodded to Tarma, who promptly exited the room. "You will become an official mentor and train the one who will take your place."

Ashley nodded. This she could do. She'd helped Tarma educate several of the other sisters. Not everyone stayed; this life wasn't for everyone. But the three that she'd helped to instruct stood around her and smiled their congratulations.

• • •

Once the meeting had dispersed, Ashley remained in the room, and for the first time she participated in an inner circle ritual. She learned a new chant and drank a new potion and welcomed the spirit of her new *raison d'être*. It was very similar to the ritual she had gone through when she first joined the sisterhood, the one her protégé would have gone through the night before.

After the ritual, Ashley visited her protégé, Nichole's, room. She couldn't wait to meet her student and teach her the ways of the sisterhood. However, after only a few minutes she worried that Nichole would be better suited to a different calling.

Nichole sat on her bed in her white gown that all the apprentices wore. Ashley still wore her maroon one. The difference in color may help her assert her authority.

The feeling of wonder permeated the room, so Ashley decided to keep it light. "How are you doing? Once you accepted the spirit and the ring, your powers emerged. You should be noticing a few subtle differences by now."

"Oh, great," Nichole replied. "It's like I'm becoming a superhero or something. Just when you walked in I could hear what sounded like a snake hissing, but that would be weird, wouldn't it? I do seem to see a glow about you. A beautiful robin's egg blue one, with green and gold flecks." Nichole cocked her head. "It kind of shimmers around you."

"Yes, and over time you will be able to recognize your sisters using their auras. Very soon you will be able to accomplish a lot more. You will be able to change your appearance." To demonstrate, Ashley shifted into a likeness of Diana Ross. "Though you shouldn't use famous people because they get a lot of attention and the goal is camouflage." She shifted back into a brunette with a heart-shaped face and blue eyes—the image she used most days. Most sisters didn't wear themselves very often. For Ashley, her own face and body reminded her too much of her life before the sisterhood. "With practice, you will even be able to change your clothes."

"Really? How does that work?" Nichole asked, her eyes wide with wonder. "I mean, like the science behind it."

For some reason, Ashley had never asked that question. All she knew was that it worked. So she answered with her best guess. "It has something to do with being able to control the atomic particles of yourself and everything around you."

"Ooh."

"This is all so you can perform the primary function of the sisterhood: removing the evil influence of men on our society."

"That sounds exciting."

"You will feel more powerful than you've ever felt before." Ashley nodded. She knew she did. "You start by evoking the prey's worst fear. When they are overcome with terror it exposes their soul—it's colored the same as their aura, but brighter. When you *see* it, use your mind and pull on the emotions that hide their true selves. Their fear, strength, and evil. It will feel like a part of you is reaching for them, like a hand you didn't know you had. You know you have it when you can taste it; every sister tastes something different. I taste ripe peaches."

"Doesn't matter who?"

"Every time." Ashley nodded. "When you taste it, you're there, and you suck all of that evil soul right out of their body." She was getting hungry just thinking about it.

"Ew."

"No, it's delicious. It gives you a delightful rush." She smiled and patted Nichole's leg until the woman smiled as well. "I always feel so energized after a harvest. So many women are saved by what we do."

"What happens to the men?" Nichole asked, still smiling but in a more forced way.

"What do you mean?" Why should she care what happened to the men?

"After you remove their souls. What happens to them?"

"They die." Ashley shook her head. "Of course."

"Do we absolutely have to kill the men?" Nichole asked in a whisper. The petite woman picked at the fringe of her gown.

"The soul is extracted. Living is no longer possible," Ashley replied, though she knew the answer wouldn't satisfy her student.

"But ... "

Although Nichole had pledged to support their mission with a whole heart she questioned their methods. Ashley started to worry about Nichole's commitment.

She held up a hand and waited a beat. Partially for the calming effect on Nichole, but also because it gave Ashley a chance to be sure her voice would hold a patience she didn't completely feel. "Would you have wanted your boyfriend to continue abusing you? Could you have left him on your own? For all the free will you had left, he may as well have tied you up. Would you have wanted him to do it to another woman?"

Nichole responded vehemently, as Ashley had predicted. "No, of course not."

The gravitas with which she spoke caused Ashley to smile. And she could see Nichole had more to say, so she waited, a level gaze firmly on her charge. Finally, the reason for the woman's contrary behavior was about to surface. Best to get it out in the open.

"It's just that ... " Nichole's saucer-like eyes met Ashley's. "Not all men are evil."

Ashley nodded. "We don't target the ones who are behaving. It's like weeding a flower garden. We only remove the plants that could harm the others."

Nichole went back to picking at her hem. "But some men change," she whispered.

Ashley wanted to shake the young woman, to tell her that men whose souls were corrupted couldn't simply clean them out again. It was only a matter of time before most men strayed down an evil path. It was their nature. But she knew from the way Nichole fidgeted she had yet more to say, so Ashley held her tongue.

"My dad changed for me." Again, Nichole lifted her huge eyes and seemed to search Ashley's face for something. "Before I was born he did drugs and messed around with loads of women. When my ma got pregnant with me he stopped all of that and became my dad."

In Ashley's experience, the male would only make that choice if it were the easiest to make. But Nichole's voice rang with love and wonder and stilled Ashley's interruption.

Nichole smiled as she rubbed at her knees. "Ma said they loved each other so much."

The emotion that poured from Nichole felt sweet and soft. In spite of herself, Ashley listened like a child to a fairy tale. She'd believed in love like that—once—long ago.

Nichole ran her hand over the fringe of frayed fabric and sniffed. "Then, one night, he was in a wreck on the way home. I was eight. Losing him broke our hearts, but Ma always told me how he'd changed when I was born. She said everybody deserves a second chance." Nichole rocked slightly back and forth, lost in memory.

Ashley remained quiet. She'd been given a second chance with the sisterhood, an out from an abusive and likely deadly marriage. A chance to help herself and women like her to be strong. How many chances did someone get?

Nichole's words burrowed into Ashley's heart. Could there be a man strong enough to fight the inherent male corruption and love her? Care for her? Live for her? In the years she'd been with the sisterhood she'd never encountered such a man.

"Nichole," Ashley said gently, "how many second chances did you give the man we found you with?"

Nichole nodded and squared her shoulders.

Still, the thought of a redeemable man tugged at Ashley's mind. Could one really exist?

• • •

The woman seemed to have more arms than an octopus. Eric Adams, private detective, disengaged himself from the grateful woman's embrace and said, "You're welcome, Mrs. Jaxon-Miller."

He'd attempted to evade her several times already; fortunately, the fifth time seemed to be the charm. Though she pouted, it seemed she got the hint and lit a cigarette instead of trying to kiss him again. She said, "Oh, no. I'm changing my name back to Jaxon. Allison Jaxon won't be associating herself with that jackass anymore."

Two days ago, she'd walked into the closet he called an office and asked him to follow her cheating husband. It had taken Eric less than an hour to snap the photos she'd just chucked across the room. Apparently, her husband cheated regularly, and in the open to boot.

A few puffs of her cigarette and the room filled with smoke. He was willing to overlook his usual no-smoking rule if it meant Ms. Jaxon was keeping her hands to herself. She dropped the half-finished cylinder into her water bottle and gave him a pointed look. "We really should talk about compensating you for your trouble."

She was slightly older, and she *was* hot. Especially in the tight miniskirt and heels that made her legs look like they went all the way up to her neck. A year ago, he may have taken her up on the offer. Back then, he'd been a ladies' man. Back then, he'd been a man.

The Bestial Butcher case ended all that. The Butcher had turned his partner on the police force, Lydia Davis, into a werewolf. A *werewolf.* Eric had barely believed her when she told him. Then, during the raid that finally brought down the Butcher, the beast ripped Eric apart in an attempt to lure Davis into the open.

Luckily for Eric, the Butcher had used his mouth to tear open his stomach, and the disease, or whatever it was that changed a human to a werewolf, passed to him. Even as the surgeons operated to close his wounds, they closed on their own.

Fortunately, the surgeon had seemed content to take the credit for Eric's miraculous recovery. The next day, the surgeon's expression was more than a little uneasy as he examined Eric's healed wounds.

Then, with the help of Lydia, Eric had checked out of the hospital the following day.

"Hey, sexy, where did you go?" Allison Jaxon was sitting on his lap, brushing the hair back from his face with one hand while working the fly on his jeans with the other.

Eric stopped himself from standing up and dumping her onto the floor. The woman needed reassurance that she was still sexy. While he wouldn't sleep with her, he could boost her ego a smidge. He caught the hand that was in his hair and moved it to his lips. "Allison, you are one of the sexiest women I've ever met, gorgeous, and successful. But you should know I can't mix business and pleasure." He lifted her from his lap as he stood and set her on her feet, grabbing her ass and leaning close to whisper into her ear, "No matter how much I want to."

Then he stepped back and let his arms drop to his sides. He was taking a chance handling her this way. He hoped he was right that she merely needed some validation. She panted, and for a moment, she looked ready to pounce. Swallowing hard, she reached into her purse and said, "I'll write you that check."

After Ms. Jaxon left, Eric tucked the check into his wallet. Private detective work paid the bills, albeit not well. Being a cop hadn't paid all that well, either. In some ways, he missed it. But after Lydia left the force to start her family, he realized it was too difficult to explain how he could smell better than any police dog. By scent alone, he could tell if a person in interrogation was lying. Unfortunately, as a cop, he had to prove it. For instance, he would have had to produce cause to search the home of the pedophile who had kidnapped that little boy even though the pervert who answered the door reeked of the child.

Eric's new partner hadn't understood when Eric barged in as the man tried to close the door. He hadn't understood when Eric punched the man into unconsciousness before the pedophile could draw the 9 mm tucked in his waistband. He hadn't understood when Eric broke through the closet wall of what seemed to be a bedroom office. As a werewolf, his strength had doubled. Of course, during the full moon, it tripled.

Eric had found the boy. Saved the day. But the questions didn't stop, and he couldn't answer them. He couldn't work on the force anymore. Not when he couldn't be honest with his own partner. No sane man would believe him.

When he talked it over with the incredibly pregnant Lydia, she understood. "I found that the only team I can really trust is family," she'd said. Then she placed a hand on his shoulder. "And you, you're family now, you know." If he ever doubted it, all he had to do was reach out with his mind. Apparently, because of the closeness of the pack, he could talk telepathically with his pack mates.

He knew, but it didn't help. He could handle being alone professionally if he had someone to come home to, to share his day with. Hell, to share the *night* with. But it couldn't be casual anymore. Wolves mated for life. Now, sex meant forever. If he wasn't careful, he could be bound for life to a complete bitch.

To anyone on the outside he appeared healthier than he ever had. Sure, he had a quicker temper than he used to, especially during the full moon. Because he'd refrained from human flesh for his first full moon, with the help of Lydia and her mate, he didn't look at humans as food. However, he now ordered his meat rare, and when the moon was full he barely cooked at all. The all-natural, raw diet cut the body fat, and the pet shampoos he used when he "wolfed out" made his hair full and shiny. Anyone who knew him thought he was happy.

The phone rang, startling him from his thoughts. A quick check of the caller ID and he answered. "Aaron Decker, how are you? How's Sin City?"

"Troubled. I could use you down here, man." Aaron sounded tired. More tired than when they'd gone through the academy together. "We've got a missing person case, juvenile, possible runaway."

"I don't know what I can do."

"That's all the false modesty you get. You were top of our class. You might have turned in your badge, but your reputation has grown in the last year. You've got instincts, and that's what we need. There's no evidence of abduction. The child left a typed note on her computer explaining she was running away, but that doesn't feel right to me. Not to mention she's the daughter of Miles Koburn, an influential man on the city council."

Politics involved, too. Geez. "Aaron, you might want to get the feds involved. Better resources—"

"You're not coming?"

The question hung in the air. He knew Aaron well, but could he work as part of a team again?

"It's an eleven-year-old girl," Aaron said. "The clock is ticking."

That did it. "I'm coming."

• • •

Ashley flipped her hair over her shoulder and strode confidently down the Strip. The dark night was lit by the ever colorful flashing lights. Other cities boasted that its citizens never slept, and although she'd never had a reason to leave Las Vegas, she was sure the nightlife here could give any of them a run for their money.

Every adult in this town focused on two things: sex and money. Women, men, young or old. All other necessities came second to the conquest of the seven deadly sins. And even these sins circled back to sex and money. Ah, but that was the good part. As the Mother taught her all those years ago, the deeper the coat of sin, the sweeter a soul.

Ashley had learned in the first few days of her own training that the sisterhood's goal was to rid the world of the evils done at the hands of men. Not every soul was as corrupt as the next, and the less tainted a man's aura, the worse the taste. Usually, after identifying those men whose hearts were mostly pure, she avoided them.

But now that Nichole had brought up the idea of a redeemable man, Ashley's eyes lingered on the less polluted specimens. The ones she used to ignore. How they held their women close. She wondered what it would feel like to be held by such a man.

She ran her nails through her hair. *Focus.* She needed to concentrate on the task at hand.

The hunt could be fun. Reading thoughts, weighing sins. Separating those indulging in a weekend of transgression from those who made depravity a way of life.

She remembered her induction and rubbed a thumb over the onyx band around her left ring finger. The ceremony, the belonging. She would never be a victim again.

Striding past the people lined up outside a club, she slid into the front of the line. She'd found prey in this club before. A wink to the bouncer at the door and she was waved through without paying the cover. He wasn't the purest man in the bunch, but as long as he remained useful he'd live. She spared a moment to wonder if the bouncer knew how close he stood to death's door.

The rhythm of the music pounded in her chest like a second heartbeat. Colored spotlight beams crisscrossed the room. She wriggled and bounced to the pulse like those around her.

She danced through the crowd, gathering her hair behind her head, and then, raising her hands in the air, she let her long dark hair fall into shoulder-length blonde curls. No one in the pulsating room noticed; neither did they notice her eyes swirl through a rainbow of colors and land on a deep, seductive blue.

Tonight, she would find prey for Nichole. The best way to learn was to do. So, after a week of orientation, Nichole would get to put what she'd learned into action. Tonight, Ashley would find Nichole's first kill.

Ashley's instincts led her to a man around fifty. Short and stocky. His thinning hair whispered of once being strawberry blond, but the bad comb-over lay limp, thin, and peppered with gray. Stretching his mouth into a vile grin, he stood at the bar and leered at the woman dancing on top of it.

The aura around the diseased leprechaun of a man swirled in dark blacks and browns. Oh, yes, he was a ripe one. Ashley strode toward him, waited until he turned in her direction, and affected a vacant expression.

"Oh." She stumbled against him and allowed her breasts to press against his arm for a moment longer than necessary. "Sorry," she mouthed at him.

"That's all right." He gripped her shoulders and moved her to stand at the bar next to him. "Let me just buy you a drink."

He waved at the bartender, and she leaned toward him again, this time catching the sweetly rotting scent of his corruption. She'd found a perfectly nasty one in the first club of the night. It seemed too easy.

The bartender passed the leprechaun her drink, and he gripped the glass by the top. If she really were the ditsy drunk blonde she pretended to be, she would have missed the little white pill he dropped into the glass. Too bad Nichole hadn't come out with her. He was almost too ripe to resist.

Giggling, she accepted the drink and downed half of it. The drug would have no effect on one of the sisterhood. She nuzzled up to his ear and yelled, as the music wouldn't allow for the seductive whisper the move called for, "I like you. How long are you going to be in town?"

"Baby," he shouted, "I gotta get back to the wife in two hours!" He grabbed her ass and pulled her closer. "I need to make this count."

"Where are you staying?" Nichole would have an easy time with this one. Her first time should be as pleasant as possible. Ashley could distract the wife while Nichole took the husband; the wife would be much better off without this jerk.

"The Palace." Short as he was, his face barely reached her cleavage. He turned his head and attempted to help himself.

She stepped away, threw her head back, and laughed, as if the Palace weren't good enough for her. She patted him on the cheek and made a show of stumbling away from him into the crowd. She felt his rage radiate at her back.

Once outside, she checked the bottle of pills she'd palmed from his coat. No label. She shook it and watched the little white tablets rattle around. Pleased that he would find no victims tonight, she emptied the pills into a nearby garbage can and then tossed the bottle in, too. Tomorrow, Nichole would ensure he would never take another victim.

• • •

Eric received the e-mail from Aaron with the tickets while at the bank depositing his check. The flight would leave first thing in the morning. Before heading home to pack, he stopped by his grandmother's house to tell her he would be out of town for a few weeks.

Her small townhouse occupied an end unit in a historic neighborhood. It had been passed to her from her parents, and she'd raised her children there. Then, when Eric's parents died in a robbery gone wrong, she'd taken him in.

The way the detectives had brought his parents' killer to justice was what led him to choose to join the force. They'd reviewed the clues, followed the evidence, and given them peace.

Although the neighborhood had gone downhill over the last twenty years, his grandmother insisted on staying in her home. No matter the crime statistics, or the fact that Eric's grandfather had had to put bars on the downstairs windows.

After his grandfather passed away five years ago Eric found himself stopping in daily. He couldn't cook, and since she made such terrific food and was on the way home, he would stop in and do a chore or two—then he would look meek and hungry. He spent many an off-hour mowing her postage-stamp-size lawn, moving furniture, or fixing things. Just his way of paying her back for the great food.

She was like a mother to him, and at seventy-one, she needed to be taken care of, though she'd never admit it. She didn't know about his transformation last year, and if he could help it, she never would.

He knew from experience that unconditional acceptance could only go so far. Years ago, he'd almost gotten serious with a woman. Unfortunately, he'd been applying to the police academy, and she was an accomplished thief. No matter what he said, she couldn't or wouldn't stop. He couldn't love someone who would cross the line he was going to defend.

He walked up the two steps to his grandmother's barred screen door. With the thick metal door open he could hear gentle singing coming from the kitchen.

Before he could knock she called out, "Come on back, dear." She never locked her doors. She refused to get a security system, but she always knew when he arrived.

"Nana," he called out as he entered and then locked the screen door behind him. "You shouldn't leave your door unlocked like that," he chastised, though he knew it would be futile. "Anyone could walk in."

"I knew it was you," came her usual reply.

"And if it wasn't me?" He followed his nose and the smell of fresh cookies to the kitchen.

She greeted him with a plate of cookies and a glass of milk. "I would ask them to leave." She pulled the plate away from his outstretched hand to emphasize her next word. "Sternly."

"I believe they'd listen to you." Eric took his plate to the little table by the bay window of the kitchen. He could see his grandmother's small garden through the glass.

The rows were perfect, like always. His nana loved to garden and had had one for as long as he could remember. The herbs seemed to stand watch by the gate, and a little flower garden was in the center. A vase on the table held some of those flowers.

The warm cookies melted in his mouth. He'd lived on his own for years, but this kitchen, this house, was home.

Nana sat at the other end of the table and sipped her mug of tea. "Will you be staying for dinner?"

"Sure." He had nothing else planned, and it only took minutes to pack a duffle.

"Are you going to tell me about your day?" she asked when their meal was almost finished.

"Nothing much to tell. I finished a case for that woman who thought her husband was cheating on her, and got paid for it." Nana hadn't questioned his choice to quit the force. And although she'd quirked an eyebrow when he started asking for his steak rare she hadn't pressed him.

"I'm very proud of you. You might have stopped being a police officer, but you still make a difference in people's lives." She patted his hand. "Are you done?" she asked, pointing to his plate.

He nodded. "Nana, I wanted to tell you, I'm heading to Vegas for a couple weeks."

"Oh, a vacation?" She rinsed the dishes and set them in the dishwasher, then brought him a bowl of green beans to snap.

"A case. Aaron—you remember Aaron?" he asked as he reached for a bean.

"Married that lovely attorney, Vivian, got a job in Vegas. Yes, I remember him. Nice boy. Loved my pot roast."

"Well, he called today and asked if I can go to Vegas to help him with a missing person case. I shouldn't be gone too long."

"I understand," she said, drying her hands on a towel and leaning a hip against the cupboard. "Be careful; I hear there are some bad eggs in Las Vegas."

"No more than anywhere else," he replied, passing her the bowl of beans. But at her arched eyebrow, an expression he knew brooked no nonsense, he said, "I promise to be careful."

· · ·

The rest of the night held many potential candidates for Nichole's first field trial, but none as delectable as the leprechaun-ish man who'd tried to drug Ashley. So she returned to the mansion.

The lush green grounds carried the scent of night blossoms and fresh mulch. Pale petals glowed under the full moon. The sisters took turns tending the house and grounds. Just because they weren't exactly normal didn't mean they didn't want to put out a good impression for the neighbors. In the 1940s, they'd opened the mansion under the guise of a women's hotel. A few years back they'd switched to simple apartments. They didn't advertise. There was no word of mouth, so no one even tried to apply for one.

Ashley crossed between the palm trees that seemed to stand guard on either side of the path. She pushed open the mansion's large wooden door, where the stone of the front porch gave way to an arching foyer. The sky mural of pink- and purple-tinged clouds painted in perpetual sunset on the ceiling seemed to ripple as she passed into the sitting room.

She heard giggling from the kitchen. She crossed the hallway, her stilettos tapping a staccato on the marble tile.

Six of her sisters sat surrounding the wood and glass table of the breakfast nook. Each woman held a spoon and passed around several pints of ice cream. The bay window behind them revealed the lights of the Strip glowing in the distance and added a festive atmosphere to the ice cream social.

Though they came from different backgrounds and different ethnic groups, they were family.

Tarma, who at the moment appeared as a long, lean woman with skin the color of caffé latte, sat opposite the door and was the first to notice Ashley's entrance. "Well, how'd it go?"

Ashley took a spoon and a pint passed to her by a short-haired redhead named Jessie. "Good." She scooped up a spoonful of dark chocolate and grinned. "Very good. Found the most delectably dark aura. He's at the Palace."

The other women moaned. Nichole wriggled in her chair. "Oh, could I have him?"

Tarma clucked her tongue. "That's rude, dear. You don't ask for a sister's prey."

Nichole hung her head as the other women nodded. But Ashley smiled at her student.

"I think we can overlook it this time, as I found him for you." She lifted a hand at their surprised expressions. "Nichole is ready. Soon, we will induct another full sister." Over a spoonful of ice cream she caught Tarma's eye. "We might have another trainee as well."

Tarma pursed her lips and nodded. "The prey has a wife?"

"Yes, but he says she's in Vegas with him. And *that* is the only thing he said that I believe," Ashley said, licking her spoon clean. "He tried to drug me."

"Sounds delicious," said Felicia, the blonde wisp of a woman with the death grip on the rocky road.

"I think he will be," Ashley said. "After spending those few moments with him I think the wife will need us."

A rustle of cloth announced the Mother's entrance an instant before she spoke. "Not every woman is meant to join us, dear."

She entered the room with an unearthly grace Ashley hoped one day to emulate. Her skin was pale and luminous, rich even in the fluorescent lights. Her long black hair didn't hint at her age, which was rumored to be over three centuries.

She swept up to the table between Tarma and Nichole, and all the women sat in reverence.

"We are a select group of women." She caressed Nichole's cheek. "You all were chosen because you have a power inside you that attracts sinful men like moths to a flame. And in consuming their dark souls you complete two purposes."

The Mother paced to the window and turned. "You provide your gift with the power it needs to thrive, and you remove the sediment of society, which, in turn, allows the women of the world to find real love." As she said this last, her voice rang out.

Ashley felt as if her heart would burst with pride for the sisterhood, for the Mother, and for their purpose. Before she recovered from the Mother's speech Nichole cleared her throat quietly.

The Mother smiled at her. "Yes, my dear."

"Are you saying we shouldn't go after him?" the quiet voice asked.

"Of course not. Ashley and Tarma will take you. It would be best for Ashley to lead you to him and for Tarma to talk to the wife." To Tarma, she said, "Assess her potential. If she is open for the gift, bring her here. If not, then console her and advise her. Either way, both of you should be ready to assist Nichole if she needs it."

Her face shining with delight, Nichole stood. "When can we go?"

They all smiled at her eagerness and then turned to Ashley. Even the Mother looked at her. The weight of Ashley's position pressed unexpectedly. She knew what was necessary, so she placed her spoon on a napkin and said, "I think we should catch them at breakfast. He had the pills, so he's obviously done this before, but he seemed to want to hide his infidelity from his wife. I say we corner him while they're having breakfast."

The Mother nodded. "I'll leave you to discuss details, then. Remember, Ashley, when Nichole releases her harvest at the ceremony you will achieve your permanent place in the inner circle." She moved from the room as gracefully as she'd entered.

Nichole exhaled as though she'd been holding her breath. "Such a commanding presence."

The rest of the women nodded and again turned to Ashley. Taking hold of her nerves and shoving them to the rear of her mind she started to lay out her strategy. The ice cream was soon forgotten.

. . .

Eric returned to his apartment and found guests. Sitting on his couch were his old partner, Lydia, and her husband. It had taken him a while to get used to the idea of them married. Things change, he had reminded himself on more than one occasion.

Lydia grinned and rocked herself off the couch into a standing position. Her belly seemed to have doubled since he last saw her. "Eric."

"Wow. How many are in there?" he joked. "You weren't kidding about starting a family." She'd never attempted to hug him before. That, coupled with the fact that it looked like she was smuggling a watermelon in her shirt, made the embrace awkward. "How are you?"

"Getting close to time." She reached a hand back to the couch for Ryan. "That's why we wanted to come by; our children are most likely to be born this moon, and we would like you to do the honors."

"Me?" He stepped back from them and checked their faces to see if they were kidding. They weren't. Suddenly, he needed a drink. Given his company, he forwent the bourbon and grabbed three bottled waters from the fridge.

"You took the course on how to deliver babies in the academy," Lydia said, opening her bottle.

True. "Yeah, but—"

"And you're one of us," Ryan said, sending a chill up Eric's spine.

True. "Yeah, but—"

"There's no one we can go to for this, Eric. What if my baby—"

"Or babies," Ryan interrupted.

She nodded. "Or babies, come out furry?" Lydia's voice broke. They really had no one else to turn to. They didn't know any other real werewolves. Any books they could find were fiction. If they went to a regular hospital pictures of their babies would be plastered all over the tabloids and social media. They really did need him.

But the full moon was in two weeks, and he was on his way to Vegas.

Lydia wiped at her face as Ryan put an arm up behind her and rested a hand on her shoulder.

"Of course I'll be there, Lydia," Eric said. "I'm flying to Vegas tomorrow, but I'll be back here for the full moon."

"Oh, thank you." She hugged him again.

This time, Ryan got in on the action by clapping a hand on Eric's shoulder. "What's in Vegas?"

"Missing person case, but it shouldn't be a problem to make it home in time."

If they'd been in wolf form, their ears would have perked. Even so, their eyes widened, and they both leaned forward a bit.

"Need any help?" Lydia asked.

Eric shook his head. "So far, it seems straightforward." Crestfallen was the only word to describe their faces, so Eric added, "But I'll call if I have any questions."

Lydia chuckled.

Ryan reddened, rubbed a hand over his face, and said, "Aside from the pregnancy, things have been a little quiet on the home front."

"Don't worry. From what I understand, you've only got two more weeks until you have all the excitement you can handle."

Chapter 2

Once Eric arrived in Las Vegas, he slung his carry-on duffel over his shoulder, ignored signs for food and gambling, and headed straight to the police cruiser just outside the glass airport doors. Aaron's e-mail had said Officer McMillan would pick him up at the airport. The delay would give the department enough time to free up a vehicle for Eric's use.

Barely three steps from the escalator a man who reeked of tequila staggered out of the crowd. As he approached, he tripped, colliding with Eric, taking them both down. "What the hell?" the man exclaimed, kicking his legs and flaying his arms.

Even as Eric disengaged his limbs from the cursing man, he patted his pocket to ensure he still had his wallet. Then the duffel tugged. A buxom, blonde woman had a hold of it and was attempting to lift it off his shoulder.

From his squatting position, Eric stood abruptly, yanked the bag, and caught the woman by the arm. "Cut that out."

"What?" She jerked away. "I was just helping you up." She huffed and flipped her shimmering hair over her shoulder as she turned away, muttering. "Try to give people a hand and this is what you get."

Before he boarded the plane he'd locked the zipper, and a quick check revealed the zip tie was still firmly in place. *Lucky for her.* He glanced in the direction the woman had gone and could see her through the crowd talking with the drunk that had tripped him in the first place. *Teamwork. Nice.*

A uniformed officer strode to Eric's side. "Are you all right?" When Eric nodded, the officer asked, "Detective Adams?"

"Yeah. Are you my ride?" He scanned the officer's badge and name tag.

"Yup. I'm Officer Max McMillan. I'm parked just over here." They walked to the curb just outside the door. Once out of the air-conditioned building Eric felt the desert heat, surprisingly not oppressive, though he suspected that would change if there were any humidity in the air.

Max lifted his sunglasses and considered Eric's expression. "It gets cooler at night."

"Good thing. If it gets much hotter, the buildings will melt."

Max laughed as they climbed in. "The sun isn't even up yet."

Before they were in their seats, a call came across the radio. "Body found, sending coordinates to onboard GPS, Lieutenant Decker requests you bring passenger to site."

"Roger, dispatch," Max responded before checking his GPS and flipping on his lights. "Looks like we have to make an unscheduled stop."

Eric grunted. The case he was called for was a missing girl, but homicide took precedence. As they drove, he fought the urge to tell Max to take him back to the airport. A missing girl he could find. She probably ran to a friend's house. A dead body required evidence, and testifying to the evidence collection at a trial. Things he already knew he couldn't do anymore.

Aaron wouldn't have insisted he come to the site unless he felt it was connected to the girl he was coming to investigate. Eric's stomach sank further. It could also be the body of the missing girl. He knew he had to see this through.

They traveled outside the city for a while; more than once, Max turned onto roads that scarcely seemed to exist. Max handled the car like he knew what he was doing so Eric stayed silent. Sure enough, they rounded a sandy hill and came to a halt behind a coroner's van.

"We're here." Max got out and waved to someone on the other side of a large stand of scrub brush. A second later, Aaron came over to greet them.

Eric climbed out of the air-conditioning and clasped his friend's hand. "What's this all about, Aaron? Is this the girl?"

"A girl. Not the one I asked you to investigate."

Eric bit back a curse. "Then why am I here?"

Aaron glanced at Max and then turned his shoulder so they faced away from the forensics team. "My gut says these two are connected. I can't say how. We have an ID on this one. Twelve-year-old Suzie Hogan. She's a runaway from a group home on a seedier side of town. Her parents are both doing time in jail. There's a notification on her file that she stopped going to school. The feds did their thing months ago, and the case is still open, but they thought she might have simply run away. Probably caught up with the wrong element."

Eric shook his head. "It fits. She runs away, thinking she can do better on her own. She can't, so she starts turning tricks and ticks off her John."

"She could have, but … " Aaron held Eric's gaze. "Something's not right here."

"And since I was in town anyway … " Eric waved his hand at the scene. "I get it." They started walking toward the scene. "When was she reported as a runaway?"

"About six months ago."

"Can we guess as to time of death in this oven?"

The team had begun packing their tools, and a couple of them chuckled. One who held a clipboard said, "Given the insect activity, I would guess more than a day, but no more than forty-eight hours ago. I should be able to give you more accurate results once she's on the table."

It appeared as if the girl's body had been literally rolled out of a car. Her arm lay crossed over her torso, and her leg was entangled in a bush of some sort. Strands of her long brown hair obscured her face. Much of it had snarled in the bush as well.

"The body isn't posed in any way," Eric said, leaning forward slightly to observe the corpse. Blood coated the dent in her right temple. The lab would most likely be able to identify a weapon, but regardless of instrument, the effect was plain. She had bruising on her hips. The mortician would be able to tell for sure, but the first guess would be sexual assault. Eric knew the others would be thinking the same. An abomination anytime, but on a young girl, it enraged him.

He struggled for composure. Thank goodness it wasn't a full moon; he wouldn't be able to hold it together. She had been broken and thrown away. Rage wouldn't help her. Nothing could now. He held his position and breathed deeply.

The scents around the body revealed themselves. Animals had been at her. They'd torn at her flesh but hadn't managed to free the leg from the bush's grip. The scent of the police and technicians hovered around the girl, but didn't actually touch the body as had those of the animals.

Under it all, he could smell the girl. Even now, there was a residual of her sweat and tears. Of her fear. He could smell her attacker. The scent of him coated every inch of her. Eric's instincts said that she had been held by him for a while. Perhaps even since she "ran away." There were others' scents too. Female. *This is bad.*

Aaron had been watching him closely, and when he straightened, the lieutenant said, "What do you see?"

Eric cocked his head, and they moved away from the bustle. "I don't think she ran away, I think he abducted her. Held her. Then, when he was done, he killed and dumped her." Gauging Aaron's expression as open-minded, Eric continued, "I also think there are others being kept where she was."

"Why do you think that?" Aaron's eyebrow raised.

"Let's call it a hunch."

"That's one hell of a hunch."

"You have no idea."

Aaron's eyes narrowed, and he cleared his throat. "Well, your hunch doesn't leave us much to go on to find the guy that did this."

"I know." Eric ran a hand through his hair. "Maybe you should call in the feds on this one? I can't give you more evidence than what you got with your gut feeling."

"We'll work it. Let the techs do their thing. Meanwhile, I'd still like for you to look at our more recent runaway case."

"That's why I'm here, but the feds should be called on that one, too."

"They've been called." Once again, Aaron narrowed his eyes. "I'll have Max take you back to the hotel—check in, grab something to eat, and I'll be by to pick you up in a couple hours."

"Sounds good." Eric glanced back at the girl's body, now being lifted into a bag. She wasn't why he'd been brought here. Even if he could find her killer the odds of him being brought to justice with Eric's help was slim to none. He wasn't a cop anymore.

...

His room at the Palace was functional. Surprisingly similar to the mid-grade room he and four other guys had stayed in during their freshman spring break in Vegas. Given its location and price he expected fancier.

The room had been thoroughly cleaned. His sensitive nose could pick up only the faint hint that other people had occupied this room before him. No fault with the maid service.

After a quick shower and change of clothes, he left the room to wander around the casino and grab a bite.

The gold and black hallway was quiet. No children fussing, televisions blaring. When Eric reached the elevator, the doors slid open, and a group of very happy, definitely drunk people stumbled out singing off-key at the top of their lungs. He stepped aside adroitly to let them pass.

One of the women began removing her top before being pulled through an open doorway, squealing. *Ah well, what happens in Vegas and all that.*

As the elevator descended the sounds from the casino increased. When the doors opened, the noise and lights assaulted the senses.

He wandered around the floor aimlessly, marveling at the supreme order behind the chaos. Waitresses in sexy, but not too revealing, uniforms walked through rows of slot machines, balancing trays of drinks, taking orders, and making small talk with the patrons.

Past the one-armed bandits, the cause of most of the flashing lights and come-hither beeps sprawled out over several levels, stood dozens of green felt tables, though only a few were open for business.

Eric scanned the crowd. Never having had an interest in gambling, and having only gotten a couple of hours' sleep on the plane, he stifled a yawn and headed toward a glass elevator and a café nestled into one corner of the upper level. Along with several tables and booths the shop also had a bar along the balcony rail so the patrons could enjoy the view. He took his sandwich and soda and sat at the rail.

From this vantage point he could see the roulette tables below him, the slots to the right, and the blackjack tables to the left.

People moved below him on the casino floor. It wasn't even afternoon, yet still the slots did a good business. He could only imagine what the floor would look like at night with patrons decked out in evening wear.

A pair of white-haired old men walked hand in hand on the far side of the roulette tables, the taller of the two caressing his partner's cheek and speaking earnestly. Eric averted his eyes from the obviously intimate moment only to watch as a rotund woman danced back from her alarming slot machine to crash into a waitress carrying a full tray.

The waitress fell gracefully to the floor, twisting to keep the glasses from toppling. She narrowly avoided having her leg crushed as the winner's mass careened toward her.

The crowd that formed around the two applauded as the waitress stood again, not having lost a drop from the drinks. Seemingly unfazed by the accident, or the attention, she balanced the tray with one hand while offering the other to the heavy woman who still struggled to stand.

Disaster averted, Eric's attention caught on a couple walking across the floor to the glass elevator as he finished his sandwich. Nothing about the couple rang out as remarkable, but for some reason he continued to watch as they entered the coffee shop.

The man walked a step ahead of the woman. Briskly, almost as if he wanted to lose her in the crowd. His strawberry-blond comb-over wisped around his head as he stomped across the floor. Matching wedding bands revealed them to be married. Rolling his eyes at the woman who followed, the man chose the table just to the left of Eric's.

Something was definitely wrong with this guy. He leered at every woman and barely seemed to notice his wife. The poor woman slouched into a chair across from her husband, defeated and apparently accepting of her husband's behavior.

Her gaze lifted from her lap and met Eric's. She flushed and straightened in her chair and ordered in a ringing voice as soon as the waitress came over.

When the man reprimanded his wife, Eric stared at his soda and silently thanked the universe that the full moon was two weeks away. Otherwise, it would be much harder to control his temper.

"I order first." The last syllable whipped through the air. The man continued in his terse tone, "You'd best remember your place. Jesus, you're just lucky I brought you on this trip."

"You're right, I'm sorry, thank you." The woman strung the words together, bowing her head again. The plea of forgiveness in her voice wrenched at Eric.

He wanted to say something. To stand up for this woman who'd quite obviously been beaten down too much to stand for herself.

Rings formed in the soda he held as he struggled to mind his own business. There was nothing illegal about treating her like dirt. But he'd get involved if the guy got physical with her, Eric promised himself.

As he breathed deeply, he heard soft female voices behind him. Eric shifted and raised his head. *Oh my God.*

Three beautiful women stood around the guy's table. They looked so amazing, Eric sipped his soda to moisten his mouth.

The drop-dead blonde stood with her back to him, seeming to whisper to the man. If Eric hadn't already been sitting, he would have needed to.

Feeling muddled, he shook his head. A brunette stood on the other side of the man, and a dark-skinned woman stood behind the wife.

The two who flanked the man wore sultry pouts and what could be called sundresses, if they had more material. They leaned over to talk to the man. From his viewpoint, Eric could see the slight curve of the blonde's bottom.

Suddenly aware of how long it had been since he'd last had sex, he tore his gaze away from the perfect bottom that peeked out at him from under the hem of her dress. *G-strings aren't underwear.* He focused on his drink.

She shifted her stance, and he felt warm—he couldn't tell if it was the heat of her skin or if he'd started to blush. Maybe he should tell her to pull down the fabric? Hell, maybe he should do it for her. A *purple* G-string.

His groin tightened. Yeah, it had been far too long. His celibacy could only extend so far; his hand longed to caress that curve.

After several seconds of concentrated breathing he turned to say something. Avoiding the beautiful bottom, he looked toward the wife's side of the table.

The dark-skinned woman wore jeans and a pastel cotton top. Instead of a sultry pout, her face held a genuine expression of concern as she laid a hand across the wife's pale one.

So intent on the words of the woman beside her, the wife didn't seem to notice when her husband left the table with the brunette.

The blonde straightened, her dress finally hiding her rear, and watched while the brunette escorted the husband out without a word or a backward glance. He groped at the brunette as they exited the café and were soon lost in the crowd of people.

The blonde shook back her long, spiral curls, caught the eye of the woman with the wife, and gave a small wave.

Eric felt himself entranced by the blonde again, his vision drinking in her athletic yet voluptuous body. When she waved, the fabric across her bosom shimmied hypnotically. Her playful demeanor changed as she turned and looked at him. Her gaze held him more than her bottom had.

"Uh, hi." *What the hell was that?* He knew how to pick up women. He needed to say something better than that.

Her eyes seemed to burn ruts into his skin as they intently swept every inch of him. He felt naked, exposed to her in every way. Closing his eyes, he still felt the heat of her gaze. He welcomed it, opened himself to it. Then it was gone.

His lids flew open only to see her back disappear into the crowd on the promenade on the other side of the glass elevator. Rushing after her, he dodged tables and an elderly couple just entering the café. He managed a few more steps before she was completely engulfed.

He went back the café. The wife and her new friend were gone. Sitting at the bar again he scanned the casino below and sipped his soda.

Who were those women? It was almost too obvious what the husband had in mind when he left, but where did the wife go? Where did the blonde go?

He stared down into the casino without seeing the people. He tried to focus on the details of the other women, but all he could think about was the blonde.

Obviously not a normal woman. A hooker? *No,* he dismissed the idea. She would have made a move on him. A John was a John, and obviously she wasn't looking for money. A member of the casino staff? Possible, but unlikely. The waitresses dressed scantily, but the blonde's dress just didn't fit in with the café's or the casino's atmosphere.

If only he hadn't been tongue-tied. Briefly, he considered contacting casino security. Maybe she was staying at the hotel. *Shit.* What would he tell them anyway? What was he thinking?

Aaron's text appeared, letting him know he was outside.

Eric stood and glanced briefly in the direction the blonde had gone. No point anyway. He buried the instinct to try to find her. Time to work.

Chapter 3

Ashley elbowed her way through the crowd, aware the man tried to follow. When their eyes had met something about him spoke to her. Not like prey. Like a tendril of white light that reached out to her.

Ridiculous. She snorted. He had the same thoughts as every man. In the seconds that their eyes met, he was consumed with lust.

She ran a hand through her hair, allowing the curls to straighten and the tint to darken as her fingers passed. Regardless of his intentions, now wasn't the time to play with him.

Nichole had taken the slimy leprechaun to a nearby hotel. They prepaid in cash for the rooms they used. Made it easier to leave, and as every day, hundreds of people got lucky at the tables, paying in cash didn't raise any eyebrows and left no trail. Especially when you could change your appearance at will.

She blinked, changing her vivid blue eyes to brown with flecks of gold.

Changing her appearance in public didn't present a risk—or at least only a minimal one. Even in the freak show of the Las Vegas Strip people moved along in their own little worlds. In fact, the larger the crowd, the less of a risk.

As Ashley neared Nichole's room she remembered how long it had taken her to perfect a public change. Even a racial change could be done in public gradually enough. She added that to her mental lesson plan. She opened the hotel room door and stepped silently inside.

Once the door closed the room was dark and quiet. The privacy drapes had been drawn. Ashley bit on the tip of her tongue to keep from calling out for Nichole. She'd expected the perfume of fear to have filled the room. Instead, only pangs of disappointment. *Damn.*

She stood just inside the doorway until her eyes adjusted to the darkness, worrying something must be wrong. She felt, more than saw, that the closets and bathroom were empty, so she stepped forward.

The bedroom came into full view. On the far bed lay the strawberry-blond man, seeming to sleep peacefully with his hands at his sides, his comb-over brushed back away from his face. On the other bed sat Nichole, still wearing her guise of the fair-skinned brunette. Her pink and yellow aura gave a slow, depressed flicker as she stared at the body of her would-be victim.

It was too early for him to be vacant; he must have gone catatonic. *Weak, little man.* He could dish out the fear, but couldn't take it. Outrage at his selfishness, of slipping so easily beyond their reach, filled Ashley. A feeling she swiftly stifled. Excess emotion wouldn't help Nichole. With cold resolve, she distanced herself from the situation.

Without a word, Ashley moved to the bed beside her protégé and patted her trembling leg gently.

After a moment, Nichole turned her head. "It was wonderful for the first couple of minutes. Then he slipped away into this. I couldn't see his soul. I couldn't take hold of his emotions." She covered her mouth with trembling fingers. "I tried to wake him. What did I do wrong?"

"It's not your fault." She patted Nichole's hand, keeping her eyes from the infuriating sight on the bed before them. "Some people can't handle fear. They just shut down. He's not dead, just trapped inside his own mind." Ashley pursed her lips for a second. "Really, the only tragedy here is that in this state his fear doesn't radiate." She stood and retrieved a couple sodas from the minibar, passing one to Nichole.

"Has this ever happened to you before?" Nichole opened her bottle and sipped slowly, watching Ashley.

Swallowing her mouthful, Ashley smiled. "Yes, actually. But as it turns out mine was a serial killer."

"Really?" Nichole shifted on the bed, bringing her other leg onto the mattress and crossing it over the other.

Pleased the mood had started to lift, Ashley continued. "He liked to kill hookers. I picked him up from a bar that used to be on 4th, Whips and Chains. He was my third, and you know the hooker angle is the easiest lure."

Nichole nodded. "Right."

"Well, his aura just oozed. I just knew I had hit the mother lode. So much so, I thought about calling Tarma so we could capture it all. I get him into the room, and no sooner does the door close than he whips out a gun." She took another drink. "I knew I needed armor, so I took the shape of the succubus."

"Wings and tail and all?"

"Every inch. I looked just like the tapestry in the Mother's bedroom. Shaping into creatures is as easy as into other people. It's just a mask. It's not you." Another sip. "I looked magnificent." She smiled, remembering how she almost distracted herself in the hotel room mirror. "Homicidal bastard fainted dead away."

Nichole covered her face again, and this time giggles escaped.

That's better, Ashley thought, then she continued. "I changed back and tried to wake him up. Nothing. I left him in the room and called the police. They came and arrested him. All of the evidence was there."

Nichole gasped. "I remember hearing about that guy. My boyfriend used to talk about him. He would complain that they shouldn't have tried him when he was in a coma."

"Yup. His DNA matched the other crime scenes, and he went to a maximum-security mental hospital." She smiled again, this time at Nichole. "I expect he'll stay there for a while."

They sat in silence, finishing their sodas. The weight in the room had lightened considerably.

"Ashley?" Nichole asked after a few minutes.

"Yes?"

"What should we do with him?" She pointed to the comatose man in front of them as if there could be a different "him" to whom she was referring. "We can't call the police."

After a moment, Ashley said, "Leave him."

"You think it's safe?"

Ashley raised an eyebrow. "You smoothed your fingerprints before you arrived." It wasn't a question. Removing the prints from their fingers was the first thing they were taught.

"Of course."

Ashley stood, tucking their empty bottles into her purse. "Leave in five minutes. Walk the Strip, find a good area, then change and go home." She touched Nichole on the shoulder. "I'll see you there." And before her nervous protégé could ask more questions, Ashley left the room.

No one could have known someone with that dark and slimy of an aura would be such a wuss. So afraid of his own fear that he receded into himself, leaving them nothing to take hold of to pull out his soul. What a waste. Leaving the body in the room left her with a residue of guilt, though she would never say that to Nichole.

Ashley hated to leave a job unfinished. As children, her brother and sister would shirk their chores for other things, but Ashley couldn't leave them undone. She would finish hers and theirs, too. Her parents never knew, and her siblings didn't care.

As an adult, she still couldn't leave things undone. It had sabotaged her career and her marriage. No, the last wasn't her fault.

She rubbed at her face as she rode the elevator down to the lobby. She'd been that woman who intimidated the men by working harder than them. Who, try as she might, could never be perfect—which her husband had reminded her of constantly. Who was another woman in another life. Tucking the memories safely away she strode out into the bright sunlight of the desert day.

She walked at a brisk pace, changing twice as she wove herself through the crowd. Given what she was leaving behind it felt best to look as different as possible. With each step, her skin and eyes darkened. Slowly. Her breasts and hips grew until the sundress stretched tight against her skin.

Once the change was complete she patted her shoulder-length hair and licked her wide lips. Pausing to look in a shop window at her reflection, she smiled. Her skin and eyes were a rich mocha.

"Oh, yeah, baby." A man stuck his bald ebony head out the window of a passing car.

Satisfied, Ashley walked to the bus stop two blocks north and caught the bus back to her neighborhood.

•••

When Eric climbed into Aaron's car he was handed a file.

"Let me handle the talking," Aaron said. "Miles Koburn has asked us to track down his daughter, but he doesn't want the media to catch on that she is a runaway." They pulled onto the freeway. "I'm going to ask her parents some follow-up questions. You should be able to inspect her room and the property, especially if you think there's a connection with the desert girl. Keep any hunches to yourself. We don't want to panic them unnecessarily."

Local politics was a game Eric didn't want to play. "They're hiding the fact their daughter is a runaway." He nodded. "How well do you know them? How would they react if Olivia had been kidnapped?"

Aaron drove away from the Strip. "He would tear the town apart, and he's connected enough that he wouldn't need to use his bare hands."

Leaning back in his seat, Eric grunted. In this city, he expected nothing less.

• • •

When Ashley got home she searched every room until she found Tarma. The lean woman sat in a rocker in the air-conditioned sunroom at the back of the house, crocheting. The setting sun cast the room with an orange glow.

Tarma created colorful blankets, spending hours working with yarn and her hook. It was a rare holdover from her days before the sisterhood. Most women inducted did their best to forget everything about their previous life. Ashley was no different.

Tarma had gone from her family's house to the sisterhood's mansion. She seemed to enjoy the fact she hadn't wasted time on relationships. And she told them on more than one occasion she'd known her purpose since childhood.

Ashley entered the sunroom and stretched out on one of the wicker chaise lounges. "Why do you crochet all the time? It's not like we need any more blankets."

"They're not for us, silly. I donate them to children's shelters." She held up the project she'd been working on, three thick rows of bold colors with a kind of ridge running through it. Beautiful work.

"Where did you learn?"

"My mother." She set the yarn, hook, and blanket into the basket beside her rocker. "It was the way she calmed down after Father was done with her."

Most of the sisters came from environments where men ruled with iron fists. Still, Ashley lowered her head as she searched for something to say. "Oh."

"Mother would make the most beautiful sweaters and blankets." Tarma looked out the window to the garden at the rear of the house. "She should have become a member of the sisterhood. She had spirit."

"It's good you have a way to remember her." Ashley couldn't remember her own mother. After trying for a while she shrugged. Any memories she would find probably weren't what she wanted to remember. The two women sat together, sharing the silence.

"Sorry," Tarma said. "I tend to lean toward melancholy when a woman won't let us help." Her hands opened and closed on her lap. Then she reached into the basket for her project. "That poor woman went home to wait for him." Her hands seemed to fly as she crocheted.

"Then it's good that he won't show," Ashley said.

Tarma smiled wanly as her hook wrapped and looped through the yarn of the blanket at tremendous speed. "I told her that, but she insisted he was really a good man, just going through a hard time since his mother died. She told me he 'followed the old school' on marriage." She looked at Ashley. "I wish the old school wasn't so bad for the women."

"No, that's not what I mean. Nichole wasn't able to take his soul."

Tarma's hands paused again. "He didn't turn her down; he was very much into her. I saw him. His aura was so dark and slimy he could have left a trail."

Laughing, Ashley leaned back in the chair again. "That's the truth. No, Nichole was just getting started when he went catatonic."

"Oh, for crying out loud." Tarma shook her head, and her hands resumed their flying maneuvers. "Well, at least she didn't mouse out. What did you do with him?"

"The only thing I could think of—we left him." Ashley ran her teeth over her lower lip. "We couldn't risk getting involved in an investigation."

"You won't be able to use those identities for several weeks you know."

"Yeah, I know. They'll want to question the women that went into the room with him." Ashley closed her eyes and concentrated on stretching every muscle. "Shame. It was one of my best outfits."

The sound of shuffling feet got Ashley's attention, and she looked up at the sunroom entrance. An old Asian woman sat on the step that led to the other room. Every feature seemed wrinkled like a raisin. Unfortunately, the sundress the old woman wore ruined the effect.

"Nichole," Tarma said gently. "You need to watch what clothes you're wearing."

The wrinkles around the old woman's eyes deepened. She looked down at herself and sighed. The struggle evident, she gave the dress sleeves and a collar.

"Better?" The old eyes looked up hopefully.

"Longer," Ashley said.

Nichole stood and again shook with effort. The dress lengthened.

Tarma made a noise that sounded like a squeaky hinge. A quick glance told Ashley the other woman was trying to muffle a giggle. "A shawl would complete the outfit."

Nichole dropped to the step. "I can't. I don't have any energy left." She leaned against the door frame. "Ashley told you?" she asked Tarma.

"Yes, she did. He was vile but also weak. Don't worry, honey, she'll take you out tonight and get you someone." She looked meaningfully at Ashley. "If you ask nice she may even start him for you."

Ashley nodded.

Nichole brightened, wrinkles smoothing away from the old face. "Oh, would you?"

Ashley felt sorry for Nichole. Such a first outing had the potential to derail her training. Not that she was slow, just lacking the instinct of most of the other women.

"Of course I will." Ashley walked to the step and draped her arm over Nichole's hunched shoulders. "Why don't you go up and get some rest? Then we'll talk about what we'll wear."

Tears filled Nichole's eyes as she stood to go upstairs. "Thank you. I'll get it eventually."

"Of course you will," Ashley and Tarma said together.

Nodding, Nichole made her way through the kitchen and out of sight.

Ashley ran her teeth across her lip again. "Tarma, can I ask you a question?"

"Always," she replied without looking up.

"Have you ever met a man that had an effect on you?"

"What kind of effect?" Tarma asked, her hands and eyes busy in her work.

"It was like he saw me." Ashley rose from the step and paced the length of the sunroom. "Not just my image, you know? The real me."

With the last statement she changed into herself. The woman she'd been before she was inducted into the sisterhood. A woman of average height, with brown eyes and dirty blonde hair, a little overweight. Nothing special.

"I doubt it. Most men can't see past the end of their nose," Tarma said, glancing up once when Ashley changed. "Seems to me there is another explanation … Were you attracted to him?"

"No," Ashley answered immediately. Was she? Something called out to her. Something connected her. "Maybe."

Tarma's hands stilled again, and she pinned Ashley with a look. "Maybe?"

Ashley tried to ignore the dryness in her mouth. She knew she could share everything with Tarma. "I don't know. I felt him looking at me when we were talking to the husband."

"I'm sure many men were looking at you." But her mentor's eyes had an edge that remained out of her voice.

"I felt him." Ashley continued pacing and wrapped her arms around her chest. "I pulled back, because I wanted the slimy bastard to go with Nichole … "

"And?" Tarma prompted when Ashley drifted off.

"I don't know what happened. I felt his eyes on me. When I turned, it was like a flash. Like I recognized him." She stood in the window. The garden had a concrete fountain that bubbled water over white marble stones. She used the rhythmic splashing as a way to focus, to calm her budding anxiety.

"You knew him from before the sisterhood?"

"No, but I knew him just the same. And he knew me. Damn, Tarma, I wanted to fall into his arms."

Tarma stopped her work and stared at Ashley with an open mouth. "That is serious."

"I know." Ashley wanted to wail but thought better of it. The whole house didn't need to know.

"What did his aura look like?" Tarma tucked away what was now half of a blanket.

"There was white." Ashley tried to remember what she'd pushed into the back of her mind. "With blue, green, and gold flecks and streaks." She felt her face start to soften and hardened her features. She couldn't let even an untainted soul weaken her. "But there was a shadow. Not a darkness … It was like nothing I've ever seen before."

"It sounds pure enough," Tarma said. "Why do you think you wanted to fall at his feet?"

Ashley cringed. "In his arms, not at his feet."

"Ashley, dear, you know it amounts to the same thing. Keep me apprised of the situation, please." Tarma hefted her basket, and with a nod, she left the room.

Was it the same thing? Ashley wouldn't serve him and certainly would never fall at his feet. Still, something about him touched her. That could not be tolerated—because she liked it and wanted more.

Chapter 4

The drive to the upscale neighborhood where the Koburns lived took about half an hour. Every now and then there would be a break between the rows of houses and Eric could see down the mountain.

On the drive, they'd passed schools and grocery stores. A park where teens were playing soccer. Normal life in normal towns. Not the image usually conjured when one thought of Las Vegas.

The Koburn home looked similar to its neighbors. A small mansion with gray-green siding and white trim, separated from the street by a large lawn framed by flowerbeds.

They said nothing as they approached the house. Eric opened his senses. Two small animals had a den under a bush by the front wall, and a snake kept watch from under a small rock.

The path to and from the front door was practically littered with scents. Without a specific target, even he wouldn't have the ability to distinguish one from the hordes of others.

They were greeted at the door by a well-dressed woman in her mid-thirties. Her navy blue blouse was both flattering and somber. Her hair and makeup were perfect. The only outward sign of her distress was the rigid way she answered the door. Eric knew she was panicked and near to falling apart. "Detective. Have you found our daughter?"

"Not yet, Mrs. Koburn. I've called in a colleague, Eric Adams"—he indicated Eric—"who specializes in missing persons."

She hesitated, as if considering the wisdom of telling someone else about their personal problems. "Very well." Two words that to any other ear would sound aloof, however, Eric heard a glimmer of hope. He hoped with her.

As the door opened Eric could see the evidence of Mr. Koburn's financial success. Marble floors, large artwork in heavy frames, and a chandelier overhead that looked wide enough to take out the three of them if it should fall.

"Mrs. Koburn, I have a few follow-up questions for you and your husband. Is he in?" Aaron asked, taking the lead.

"And I suppose Mr. Adams needs to see her room." She stood with her hands listlessly by her sides, exhaustion marking every inch of her.

"It would help. Yes, ma'am," Aaron replied.

Her gaze burned into Eric. Angry and frightened for her daughter, she had very little control, and Eric knew she was fighting against the urge to scream at them to stop wasting time and that even exhausted she was ready to begin house-to-house searches on her own.

Eric kept his expression soft while he said, "I believe I can help."

They remained in their positions for a moment before she rolled back her shoulders and looked pointedly at Aaron. "You know the way to Olivia's room, please show him up. I'll find Miles." As she strode away the crack her heels made against the marble echoed through the vaulted room.

Eric arched an eyebrow at Aaron, who shrugged. "She's used to being in control, and now she has none." Aaron led the way up the massive staircase. "The bedrooms are this way. Olivia's faces the back; her parents' is across the hall on the front."

At the top of the stairs Aaron turned left.

"What's to the right?" Eric asked.

"Upstairs living room, guest bedroom, and a private office. I got the full tour when we came here the first time." Aaron turned right and entered what Eric assumed to be Olivia's bedroom, but once they were inside he saw no sign of a bed.

"This is her living area." Aaron motioned to the desk and shelves of books. "Her bedroom is through here."

Now this looked like a little girl's room. An entire wall of white shelves held dolls and figurines. All of the wood in the room had been painted white. The curtains, throw rug, and bedspread were done in the bright colors of Easter and little girls.

Nothing in the room seemed out of place. No stray dishes or clothes. No toys strewn about. It felt safe to assume when you grew up with someone else putting your things away, if you wanted privacy, you learned to do it yourself. "When you talk with the parents, ask if they've had the room cleaned in any way since she left."

"We haven't." The man that stood in the doorway wore a suit. A black tie was knotted at his throat. "I'd appreciate it if you can make this quick; I have business associates downstairs."

"I understand," Aaron said. He quickly introduced Eric to Mr. Koburn. "Let's talk in the sitting room."

"Not even to vacuum or dust?" Eric asked as they filed into Olivia's sitting area.

"No," Mrs. Koburn said. "Maria doesn't come until tomorrow."

Eric turned back to the room. If the others were watching him it might appear as though he was simply staring. Of all his new abilities, his incredible sense of smell was by far the most useful in this situation. He breathed deeply, feeling the scents of everyone who'd been in the room. He moved slowly, leaning toward her closet and then the bed. Both were places where the girl's fragrances would be prominent.

He began to separate and identify the smells. The girl and what was most likely the housekeeper permeated the entire room. There were others of course—her parents, Aaron, and even officer McMillan, most likely from when they first investigated the girl's disappearance.

But there was something else. Another scent on the bed. The closer he leaned, the stronger the scent. Stepping to the edge of the bed Eric donned a pair of gloves. Like the pictures of women's beds in every advertisement he'd ever seen, the head of the bed was loaded with pillows, including two fancy ones outside of the comforter. He carefully moved these to the end of the bed. Then he pulled back the quilted cacophony of pastels.

The sheet set was light pink, as were most of the pillows. Tucked under the sheets, resting its head against the mountain of pillows, was what appeared to be a ragdoll in pink pajamas.

The doll itself seemed to be of simple construction. Two pieces, front and back, with arms and legs jutting out from the body like a gingerbread man. The face appeared to be drawn on by a marker. Odder still were the clothes. Pink and silky, certainly cleaner than the body of the doll, with seams on the outside as if stitched in haste.

What's more, the doll smelled very little like the rest of the room. It was newly introduced. He'd bet it had never been washed in the family's laundry. Until he talked to the Koburns he didn't want to move it, so he leaned in and sniffed, then moved about the room to track the scent.

Sure enough, the scent traced a line across the floor to a dresser topped with an ornate mirror in one corner of the room. Then it went through glass doors to a balcony. His stomach sank. However the abductor had managed it, he'd left with the girl this way.

As Eric turned from the doors he heard a throat clear behind him. Aaron and the Koburns were standing in the door. "Mr. and Mrs. Koburn," he began after he got the nod from Aaron, "are you familiar with all of your daughter's toys?"

Mr. Koburn shrugged and shook his head, but his wife nodded. "Most of them, yes. She received an allowance for little chores so she bought a few on her own. She liked to show them to me, though."

Eric nodded. "Without touching, can you tell me if the doll on the bed is familiar to you?"

She leaned over. "I've never seen that before in my life." She straightened, eyes wide and wild, and wrapped her arms about herself, as her husband leaned in for a look.

Mr. Koburn scowled. "What does this mean? Did she run away? She left a note. Where did that come from?" He looked at Aaron then back at the doll. He whispered, "Was she kidnapped?"

Eric removed an evidence bag from his pocket and, using his gloved hand, tucked the doll into it. "We're not sure."

Aaron said, "I know you have business associates here, but we would like to have our forensics team come by and process this room." Mr. Koburn nodded, his hands clenched, his jaw set.

"There is still a chance she ran away?" Mrs. Koburn asked.

Aaron shook his head. "There's a chance, but in my opinion, it's a small one. I think we should look at this like a kidnapping until we know it's not."

"But the note … " Tears welled in Mrs. Koburn's eyes.

"Notes can be forged," Eric said.

"Of course they can." Mr. Koburn frowned. "We should have looked at it this way from the beginning. I'm sorry." Eric couldn't tell if he was talking to Aaron, his wife, or his missing daughter. To Aaron he said, "Call your team. My associates are leaving now."

· · ·

The afternoon came and went. Twilight deepened into night. While the forensics team swept the room, Aaron and Eric checked the backyard. Olivia's bedroom balcony attached to a system of balconies and decks that led to the yard. The lawn was bordered by a short rock wall. Beyond that, the hillside sloped to a road below.

Eric paced the rock wall. Her scent was here; the kidnapper's had to be as well. Days had passed since she was reported missing. Winds had blown. Animals had crossed the trail. Still, he had to find something. The kidnapper would have had to crawl over the wall, taken his time, stayed down. Eric knew if he wanted to find a scent this would be the place to do it.

Finally, something caught his attention behind a garden of ornamental grass. He'd stooped to get a good whiff and saw a slight indentation in the dirt when Aaron tapped him on his shoulder. "Hard to find something in the dark."

"Yeah." Eric cleared his throat. "Do you have a flashlight?"

Aaron grunted, clicked on a small LED light, and handed it over. "I heard you sniffing."

"Hay fever," Eric said. Aaron obviously didn't want to let this go, but maybe he could be distracted. "I've got a partial shoe print. I think he took this route over the wall."

Using his radio, Aaron called someone over to take a cast of the print. They looked for fibers or any other signs of the kidnapper's passage and found nothing.

"Did you get a list of Miles Koburn's business associates?" Eric asked. The cold trail irked. He'd expected to find some other evidence, something else that would allow him to find this girl.

"And the service people," Aaron confirmed. "The Koburns' as well as their neighbors'. You know the feds are automatically notified on kidnappings. They arrived while you were scoping out the hillside."

"Are we off the case?" Eric stretched and crawled over the wall down the hillside to the road below. No skid marks.

"No, not entirely. We have a good relationship with the local office. They're keeping us in the loop. We just have to do the same." Aaron scratched his cheek.

"No reason to follow the same leads." Eric inspected the side of the road. Gum, cigarette butts, and bits of glass, but that was all.

"Exactly. They're having their lab work on the shoe print and the doll." Aaron made a note on his tablet.

Eric's gut said the normal avenues—interviews with the girl's school friends and knocking on doors at ten o'clock at night—wouldn't work. And the regular service people wouldn't have taken a child from the homes where they were employed. But the interviews had to be done, and the sooner they got started the better.

After hours talking to neighbors, weepy little girls, and irate parents, they headed back to the car. Eric stifled a growl. "It always feels like a waste of time asking questions of people who know nothing."

Aaron said, "It's late. I'm starving and could use a drink. What do you say?"

"I'm in," Max said, jogging up from behind them.

He hadn't exactly been invited, but Eric caught Aaron's eye and shrugged. The animated young cop might distract from the fact that they had to wait for tests to come back before they could hope to save the girl.

"Fine," Aaron said, clapping Max on the shoulder, "but you get the first round."

"As long as I get to pick the place," Max said.

"As long as it has food," Eric agreed.

• • •

It was a club off the Strip called The Layer, and according to Max it was the hottest new bar in town. The outside looked like a warehouse. As they pulled in, the only tip-off that it housed a club was the line of people wrapped around the building.

"Looks like there's a wait," Eric said, getting out of the car. "I'd rather eat fast food than wait in that line."

"Don't worry, we'll get in." Max led the way with a swagger. Eric and Aaron exchanged smirks behind his back as they followed. Max had already proved entertaining.

To one side of the door stood a woman in a black leather pantsuit holding a clipboard. On either side of her stood two extremely large men. "Obviously hired for their personality," Eric whispered to Aaron as Max walked up to the woman who had just waved a couple more people inside.

Max placed a hand on the small of her back and whispered in her ear. After a second, she flipped her dark red hair back, looked all three men over, and smiled.

Reaching into her very low-cut blouse she removed a business card and handed it to Max with a wink.

Max nodded to her, tucked the card in his pocket, and led the way into the club.

"Do we want to know what you said to her?" Eric asked once they'd picked out a table to the right of the large dance floor.

Max grinned. "No."

Aaron asked, "Will I have to arrest you?"

Max's smile remained as he waved a waitress over.

"What'll it be, boys?" The waitress seemed to be wearing a form-fitting tuxedo, but once Eric looked closer he realized it was body paint. All she really wore was a small string bikini.

They ordered a pitcher of beer and a pizza.

"Are you attached, Detective?" Max asked Eric.

"Married to the job."

"Then here's to open relationships," Max toasted, and the other two lifted their beers in response.

"Vivian is understanding about the job that way," Aaron said of his wife. "Speaking of Viv, you know you can't leave town without coming by the house to say hello."

"I will," Eric said. "Even so, I can't stay in town long. My old partner got married and is having a baby. For some reason, she wants me to be there when she delivers."

"When is she due?"

"Two weeks. I hope we find Olivia before then."

The three of them sat in silence for a while before Max cleared his throat. "In the spirit of open relationships," he picked up where he'd left off, "I've got a game for us to play." Max rubbed his hands together. "We take turns picking women for the other to get their numbers. Aaron, your relationship is as open as Viv will allow, so you keep score. We each have five minutes to get a phone number."

"If we don't get it?"

"You do a shot of whiskey," Max replied.

Aaron let out an exaggerated "ooh."

Max laughed. "It's actually a good thing. The more you drink, the more you relax. The more relaxed you are, the more likely you'll get phone numbers." Max sipped his beer regally. "Now, who to send you after first … "

"Her in the green." Aaron indicated one of three women who had just sat down from a turn on the dance floor.

Eric took a sip and stood. "Wait, what happens when I get the number?"

"Then I take a shot of whiskey," Max said.

"The idea is for us to just get drunk then." When Max nodded, Eric chuckled and made his way over to the table. He'd had a high tolerance for alcohol before he became a werewolf. Now, poor Max didn't stand a chance.

"Good evening, ladies," he said when he stood at their table. "My friend over there dared me to get your phone numbers. So, would you mind if I joined you?"

They studied him warily, but one waved him to a seat. Max was going to get very drunk.

The women watched him as if he were about to pounce. He smiled and touched the hand of the woman on his right. "I'd rather leave you in peace, but my buddy over there thinks I have a problem picking up women."

The woman on his right leaned toward him. "I doubt that." She moistened her lips and ran her thumb across his index finger. "I'm Jean."

"Yeah, well." He placed his other hand on top of hers and smiled at her friends. "If I came back with all three of your numbers I'd be off to a good start."

"I'll bet you would." The one on his left, not nearly as inebriated as her friends, looked him over closely.

"Amanda's our DD," Jean said, disengaging her hand and scribbling on a napkin. "It's even my real number."

"That's great. Thanks." He took the napkin from her and raised an eyebrow at the other two, breaking out a charming expression that he used to use with his nana to get extra dessert. "Please."

"Oh, God, don't beg." Amanda wrote a number down and passed it to him, the hint of a smile playing on her lips.

The last woman leaned over the table to run her napkin over his lips. "Mine's real, too." Her dress dipped to expose impressive cleavage. "Everything's real."

"I'll keep that in mind." Eric smiled at each of them then left, very much aware he was being watched as he walked back to his table. He couldn't help but chuckle at the women's giggles.

Aaron grinned at Eric. "They were looking at your ass."

Ignoring him, Eric counted each napkin as he put it down in front of Max. "That's three." He waved to a passing waitress. "My friend here will need three shots of whiskey, and please leave the bottle."

"That was too easy," Max said.

The waitress set the three shots in front of Max. Then another arrived with their pizza.

Eric slid a hot slice from the pie. He nodded to Aaron and before the second bite said, "It's good."

Aaron chuckled. "Maybe we'll need some hot wings, too."

Over the course of the evening Eric did well but struck out enough that even he felt a little fuzzy. When he came back to the table after trying to get the number of a thin, short-haired redhead he had to admit he was having fun. "Even the 'my friends are daring me' didn't work with her." Eric threw back the waiting shot. "She's a lesbian."

"You don't know that," Aaron said, munching on a buffalo wing.

"That's what she told me." Eric picked up a wing and watched Max with interest.

Already wiping his mouth and popping a mint, Max stood. "You didn't ask right." He smoothed his clothes and sauntered over to the redhead.

Eric shook his head mournfully as he watched his new friend.

"You think she's really a lesbian?" Aaron asked.

"Oh, yeah." Eric was already feeling sorry for Max. "See that large blonde woman coming up behind him?"

"Oh no."

The large woman topped Max by a foot and a half. She placed a hand on his shoulder and apparently squeezed, because his face contorted in pain as he jumped and grabbed his shoulder.

Though his back was to Eric, he knew Max would be talking fast.

Eric sipped at his beer, trying to dilute the whiskey coursing through his system. "Twenty bucks says he gets their numbers."

Aaron studied the trio for a moment and agreed to the bet. "That blonde looks like she's going to crush him."

They spent another minute intensely watching the action and when the two women kissed Eric felt his blood heat. The redhead passed a napkin to Max and the women whispered to each other as they watched him walk away.

"And that's how it's done." Max placed the napkin on the table displaying the women's names and number.

"Damn." Aaron smacked the table and dug out a twenty.

"You bet against me." Max tsked. "Everybody likes a little variety."

Grinning, Eric toasted Max with the shot as he tucked the twenty in his pocket. The man was just too good. Eric had participated in a threesome once, back in his younger, more carefree days. Now, though, he needed more than a conquest. The game had been fun, but he knew he wouldn't call any of the numbers in the stack in front of him.

Aaron counted up napkins. "You're tied."

"Okay, man, tiebreaker time," Max said. He gestured toward the bar's entrance. "Two Latina babes just walked in. You have to get numbers for both of them. Damn, lucky bastard, they're twins."

Eric turned and looked. It took a moment to sort through the crowd, but he soon caught sight of the women, tall and attractive. Tan skin glowed in the lights, and long black hair fell straight to the middle of their backs.

"Okay, I got this." Eric stood and straightened his shirt.

He weaved his way around the tables, and as he neared the twins he reached out a hand to tap the closest on the shoulder. Then it was like he'd been smacked. This woman smelled similar to the blonde with the purple G-string at the casino earlier. No. No, it *was* her.

She had changed her appearance. How did she do that? His hazy mind worked on that a bit. She was supernatural—she must be—but what kind? Not that he cared, really. Still, it put her in another class altogether. It didn't hurt that she smelled amazing.

Before he could touch her shoulder, she turned. He let his fingers rest lightly on her shoulder, then glide down her arm. "Hello." His voice felt thick. His breath came fast. Never in his life had he reacted to a woman this way, except maybe when he was eight.

"Hi," the other woman responded, grinning at him. The color of her eyes seemed to spin.

Eric shook his head, the alcohol affecting him worse than he thought possible. He was seeing things. "Um, I'm Eric." He reached out his hand to the other one.

"Nichole," she said, then got an elbow and grunt from her twin. "Sandra Nichole. As she shook his hand, she turned to stare at her sister. "Uh, *Dana*, why don't I get us a table?" She turned back to Eric. "Nice meeting you."

Eric nodded at the retreating back and then turned to the woman who'd been in the corner of his mind since that afternoon. "I'm glad to see you again."

Eric could see something like panic in her eyes. "What are you talking about?" She wrinkled her nose. "I've never met you before."

Chapter 5

She fought the urge to moisten her lips. How could he know? She recognized him, of course, the man from the café that afternoon, but there was no way he could recognize her. Why would he say that? Was it a line he used to pick up women? She remained quiet, waiting for him to speak.

A moment passed, and he continued to smile at her. He could at least have the decency to look uncomfortable. She scanned the room. "Well, if that's all then."

His expression changed like lightning. "Wait." He moved to grip her arm and stopped inches from her skin.

Even a person unaccustomed to reading emotions could sense he earnestly didn't want her to walk away. To Ashley, he may as well have shouted it. She couldn't fathom why he wanted her to stay so desperately.

Pleased to have maintained the advantage, and filled with curiosity, she clasped her hands in front of her and waited, allowing the corners of her mouth to twitch only slightly when he groped for something else to say.

When he did speak his voice seemed to rumble. "Want a drink?"

Unable to hold it back, she grinned and nodded once. Following him to a table, she rationalized the distraction. Nichole would be fine and perhaps better off without someone over her shoulder. Perhaps, if Ashley dealt with a less ripe man, it would help her maintain her edge. A bit of practice.

The table held several nearly empty food baskets which he stacked and pushed off to the side. Enjoying watching him squirm, she raised an eyebrow and leaned back. He shifted and waved for a waitress, tapping a staccato on the table while they waited.

After a moment, a waitress appeared and took their orders for white wine. Watching him carefully, Ashley could tell he had matched her order and wished she'd chosen something else. *Ah, too bad.*

"So," he croaked. He cleared his throat and then spoke again. "Are you visiting Vegas?"

Small talk. Easy. "No, I live here." Easy but boring, and no reason not to play. "So, what about this weather?"

"Um, yeah, it's hot," he said. She watched his brow crease as he seemed to struggle for something else to say. Running a hand through his hair he sighed. "I don't have anything amazing to say."

"Really?" The sarcastic comment came out without a thought.

"Really." He delivered his answer with such direct honesty she fought the impulse to giggle.

No, no giggling. She straightened her curving lips. What was she doing? She shouldn't be sitting with him; she really should be with Nichole.

Thinking of her student, Ashley glanced around, found the woman standing at the bar, and caught her eye. Instead of the bundle of nerves Ashley expected, Nichole grinned, waved, and gave her a thumbs up. Ashley dipped her head, pinching the bridge of her nose. "She thinks I'm going to get lucky," Ashley muttered.

"Your … sister?" The man across from her glanced around.

"Never mind." Ashley regained his attention. "What's your name?"

"Eric Adams. What's y—" The obvious question was interrupted by the waitress and their wine.

"Dana," Ashley answered when the woman walked away.

"Dana … ?" He dragged the word out, motioning with his glass, waiting for her last name.

"Eric, what is your intention here?" Suddenly, she felt impatient. She'd become distracted, which had of course distracted Nichole.

This man was entertaining and surprisingly attractive. An observation she never thought she could make. Waiting for him to get to the point could take all night, and she had things to do.

"Intention?" His brows furrowed, and he lifted his glass to his lips.

"I'm not interested in a business proposition," she said.

He smiled over his glass.

"And I'm not interested in a personal relationship, either."

He set his glass down.

His disappointment was palpable, and her stomach twisted in response. It didn't matter. His feelings were inconsequential, she reminded herself. As were hers. She had a responsibility, and she'd wasted too much time indulging her curiosity.

"You want to go back to your friend." He did nothing to hide the regret in his voice.

He'd said "friend." They were disguised as twins. How could he know? She carefully schooled her features to hide her discomfort. As she rose, she said, "Sister. And I've abandoned her to sit with you."

"I understand," he said. Also standing, he stepped around to her side of the table and pleasantly extended his hand.

She took it, planning to shake it briefly, but he closed the distance between them with a step and slipped his free arm around her waist. Their joined hands pressed between them.

His movements were so unexpected she didn't have a chance to react before he leaned in, lightly brushing her lips with his, and then let her go. But he didn't step back.

"I'd have killed myself if I hadn't done that," he said, his lips inches from hers.

Her body reacted. Heat. Her face felt hot, and something seemed to ignite inside her. Things awakened; every nerve felt alive for the first time. Incredible. Intriguing. Infuriating. Damn him.

Still gripping his hand she twisted, swept her right leg behind his, and stepped closer, tripping him backwards onto the floor. She released his hand and pointed a finger in his face while placing one high-heeled shoe on his crotch.

"You didn't have permission to do that." The venom behind her words was lost when she realized he was still smiling.

"You have beautiful legs."

Though this man confused her, she maintained her hard expression. "This is a warning." He didn't fear her, but he didn't want to possess her, either. Every way she knew to control the situation was gone.

"Yes, of course." He remained on the floor, propped on his elbows as if it were the most comfortable speaking position in the world. "I would like to see you again. Maybe when you're not out with your *sister* … " He curled his fingers in air quotes around the word "sister."

"Perhaps you will. You said you've done so already." She removed her foot and stalked off to find Nichole.

And found her deep in conversation with a waitress. "Are you ready to go?" Ashley asked.

"Yeah, sure." Nichole looked from Ashley back to the waitress. "Thanks for the information." She handed the woman a twenty.

Once outside in the night air they both spoke at once.

"So how'd it go?"

"Why'd you pay her?"

Giggling a little, Nichole answered first. "The waitress was talking to a bartender and bouncer about a guy that comes in every Tuesday and harasses her." They climbed into their car. "Big tipper, but he's getting annoying, and she feels uncomfortable now."

"So you bought his description?" Amateur mistake. "You didn't need to pay her. You just come back on Tuesday and look for him."

"I didn't know what he looked like."

Ashley pulled out of the lot and silently called to the universe for patience. "You can see his aura. If he's prey, you'd be able to pick him out of the crowd, even if he were dressed as a woman or hiding in a box."

"Right." Nichole sounded like she was pouting, but Ashley refused to look.

"I'm trying to help you," Ashley said with an even tone.

"But there were no ripe ones there."

"The night is still young." They pulled into the parking lot of another club. Ashley undid her belt and was out of the car before she realized Nichole hadn't moved.

"What are you waiting for?" She ducked her head to see into the car.

"How did it go?" Nichole asked.

"How'd what go?"

"The talk with your new disciple. He seemed to want to worship you."

Ashley chuckled and closed the car door. If Nichole wanted an answer she'd have to get out too. It worked.

"Well?" Nichole asked, slamming the car door.

"Nothing special."

"He kissed you." They walked across the parking lot.

"Yes, and now he knows better." She fought to stay irritated, but the remaining warmth of the kiss and the memory of Eric grinning up at her from the floor made it a losing battle.

"Did you like it?" Nichole rubbed her hands together. "Did he ask you on a date?"

"Who do you think we are?" Ashley snapped. "We don't date; we no longer *need* men." Best that she remember that, as well. "I was curious as to what he wanted. That's all." Ashley decided then that the best way to battle the memory was to ignore it altogether. "We have a purpose tonight."

"I know." Nichole rubbed her hands together again. "All right, let's go find some scum."

After a few moments in this club, they located several ripe men. But one, in a large cowboy hat and with a wrestler's build, positioned against a wall near one of the side bars, stood out most.

They kept their Latina guises and chose seats at the center bar. Over several hours, they watched him and who he approached.

He was buying drinks for girls too young to be in the club in the first place. He was hunting too. Finally, one of the young women giggled to her friends and kept looking in his direction. The hunter grinned, not in excitement like his quarry, but in satisfaction.

Nichole and Ashley exchanged a glance. The hunter had found his prey. And they'd found theirs. With a nod to Ashley, Nichole moved off to the ladies' room to change her appearance. He would be hers so she would be the lure.

Ashley stayed in place and in her current form and watched the girls move closer to the hunter. Gazelles, not realizing they were being stalked.

With her friends surrounding her, the hunter's target remained safe. Separated from the herd she'd be easy pickins. The way she kept looking in his direction, she seemed to be waiting for his signal to approach, ready to break away at any moment.

The hunter pushed away from the wall. Crap, the bastard didn't waste time. Even as she moved to intercept the girl Ashley scanned the crowd for Nichole. She finally spotted her, in the form of a petite blonde, wide-eyed and well-endowed, just leaving the ladies' room.

Nichole only needed another minute or two, so Ashley retrieved a discarded, half-full glass and bumped into the innocent girl, dumping the dregs of a strawberry daiquiri down the front of her blouse.

"Oh, crap, I'm sorry." Ashley slurred her speech and swayed, grabbing a napkin off a nearby table to dab at the blouse.

"Oh my God!" The girl fanned her hands in the air and backed away from Ashley's napkin.

The girl's friends surrounded her immediately and ushered her off to the bathroom. Ashley stumbled up to the nearby bar and ordered a daiquiri to keep in character. She didn't want to tip the hunter off.

Then she heard Nichole make her move. Did he have the time? Ashley nearly flinched, the line was so transparent, but then any line delivered with vacant wide eyes was believable.

Ashley turned and leaned against the bar. With peripheral vision, she watched Nichole talk to the hunter, yelling in his ear and occasionally giggling when he yelled in hers.

All that was required of Ashley now was to watch and wait.

• • •

Once back in his hotel room Eric sat at the small table by the window. The evening had been a great way to blow off steam. He hadn't had a night with the guys in ages. Mostly because once he'd left the force he didn't feel right going to McDaniel's, the local cop bar.

He glanced at the desk with the work folders on top. Then at the large empty bed. The bed reminded him he was alone, which in turn gave him an image of the woman he'd met at the bar. She was human, but also something more. She intrigued him, more than any case he'd ever worked.

At one time in his life he would have been attracted by her beauty. Her smile. Her eyes. Knowing that her looks weren't the real her, he struggled to determine what caused his instant attraction. Her scent? The way she seemed to see into him? Whatever it was, he needed to forget her. A supernatural woman with far too many secrets, he would never be able to trust her. Nothing good could come from that woman.

Chapter 6

Ashley sipped her daiquiri and studied the club. A large dance floor surrounded a central bar and was packed with couples gyrating to the pace of the music.

One of the blessings of the sisterhood was that alcohol and other deleterious substances had no effect. On some nights, Ashley would have given her right arm to be able to numb her mind and drift like the humans around her. Like she used to.

When she'd been mortal she'd drunk. In the beginning, she did it to feel warm and fuzzy. Just a way to relax and unwind. But then after she got married it became a way to escape. Her husband hadn't been an ass when they met. He was strong and possessive, but in that decade, that behavior was romantic and not the warning sign it was now. Drinking had been a comfort then. A hug when she had no other way to get one.

Since the sisterhood, she only drank to blend in with humans, to play the part expected of the prey to the slime she hunted. Most of the time she didn't miss the effect. Occasionally, about once or twice a year, she would sip a cocktail for herself, remembering the warm and fuzzy effect fondly.

Ashley sipped again, glancing at Nichole. She leaned against the wall while the hunter braced his elbow beside her head, leaning in to speak almost directly into her ear.

They should be leaving soon. Ashley reminded herself she'd taught Nichole well. Taking too long made it too easy for people to notice you and try to help.

After another ten minutes, Ashley was still anxious. Nichole needed to step up the pace. So, Ashley sat her glass down and strolled toward the exit, catching Nichole's eye as she went. A clear sign *it's time to go*.

The night air felt good on her bare arms. Brisk. Almost as if the air passed along energy with the modest chill. She got in the car and started it. She barely noticed the music on the radio even as she tapped her fingers to the beat. Nichole should bring the hunter out any minute. Meanwhile, her mind wandered.

Eric. What was up with him, anyway? He knew they weren't sisters, but he couldn't see through her disguises. No one could. He'd have to be able to see her true self. Her aura. And that was impossible for a man, or so her teachings in the sisterhood had taught her.

Nichole emerged from the club with the hunter's hand possessively around her neck. *Well, finally.* He steered her to his black SUV and opened the door for her. When he walked to the other side of his car Nichole grinned at Ashley and twiddled her fingers.

Ashley smiled at her protégé's excitement. Nichole should be eager; this guy looked tasty. A child predator. There was no greater sin than to taint the innocence of youth.

Ashley pulled out of her space and followed them. They drove toward the Strip, passing the club where she'd met Eric.

Without thinking, Ashley felt for him, to sense his presence. A pang of disappointment hit her. He'd left. Maybe he'd gone home with his friends. Or a woman. He was plenty attractive.

She shook her head. He could do anything he wanted. She had no claim to him. The hunter's black SUV changed lanes, and she followed suit to keep them in sight.

There was always the possibility Eric had gone in search of her. The stray thought lifted her spirits immensely. But the grin on her lips only lasted a moment. What was wrong with her?

She pushed her self-examination to the side when they drove out of Vegas and onto the desert highway. Not wanting to give herself away Ashley cut her lights and navigated by the glow of Nichole's aura bouncing along in the vehicle ahead of her.

By now, any normal girl would be getting nervous, with the lights of civilization only a glow on the horizon. No one around for miles. No one but cacti and coyotes to hear her scream. He'd done this before. He probably had a favorite dumping place as well.

If this were her show, instead of Nichole's, she'd make him live the terror of his victims. Fair punishment for any crime. But this wasn't her show; every sister had her own way of drawing out the fear. Nichole was calling the shots tonight, and Ashley's job was simply moral support.

The car ahead of her veered sharply right beyond a stand of scrubby little bushes and stopped.

Not wanting to warn him with the sound of her vehicle Ashley stopped, too, and waited.

The hunter got out and walked around to the passenger side, opening the door and yanking Nichole out by the hair. He pulled her away from the road, far enough onto the packed earth for Ashley to see clearly.

"Okay, lay it on him," Ashley whispered under her breath.

The hunter slapped Nichole across the face so hard she fell to her knees. She sat, head bowed at the hunter's feet. When he took off his belt Ashley cringed, waiting for Nichole to do as she'd learned, to twist the fear from him.

"Come on." Ashley gripped the steering wheel and leaned in. "Do it. You can do it."

But Nichole didn't move, even when the first blow came down from the belt. And another. *Damn.* Another. Nichole's aura dimmed.

"Oh, damn." Ashley got out of the car and strode toward the hunter. "Enough!" she roared.

His head snapped up, and a nasty grin contorted his features. "I'll save her for later." He stepped around the still hunched

Nichole. "I'm gonna make you scream." He took both ends of the belt in one hand and snapped it.

The move was obviously meant to intimidate, but his complete ignorance of the current situation struck Ashley as funny, and she laughed out loud.

"What are you laughing at, bitch?" He swung the belt against his boot. "I'm going to fuck you. Then I'm going to gut you."

This brought a fresh wave of laughter.

"With your belt?" She stood still, waiting for him to get in close. "You're a moron if you think I'd be scared by a little dick with a belt."

Dropping the belt, he lunged at her with both hands. She stepped adroitly out of the way, allowing him to crash to the parched ground.

"No wonder you prey on children." She kicked a loose rock at him.

When he tried to stand she reached out her mind and touched his. Time to draw out his fears. She sifted through memories of his victims as if she were searching for just the right app on a phone.

After a second, he tried to get up, and she placed her stiletto in the small of his back and said, "No, don't get up."

He'd taken his first victim as a teenager. A hooker then, older and not his type, but it gave him a taste. Ashley took the pleasure he felt at her torture and death, twisted it to fear, and changed his perspective.

He cried out, waving his open palms in the air. The sound was a combination of a howl and whimper. Scrambling at the dirt, he wailed, "I'll do anything you want, just don't kill me."

Ashley twisted the memory of his next victim, a classmate in high school. He screamed again, his voice rising an octave.

Fear ran off him in rivulets. She twisted again and again. Like juicing an orange, she wanted to be sure she got every drop.

Finally, he lay on the ground whimpering. She prepared for the final blow, to remove his soul.

"Wait." Nichole stepped into view.

"You want to finish him? I think there's a little left," Ashley said, glad to see her student come back on her own.

"No, I want you to let him go now." She laid a hand on Ashley's arm.

"What are you talking about?" Ashley stared at Nichole. "You wanted to finish him an hour ago." Ashley studied the woman she'd been training for the past few months. "Do you feel guilty? Did he get to you?" She patted Nichole's shoulder. "Some sisters relive their own past on their first time out. It's nothing to worry about."

When Nichole said nothing, things became clear.

"You feel sorry for him. You want me to spare him." Aghast, Ashley nudged the barely moving man with her toe. "You didn't see what he has done."

"Doesn't matter. Whatever he's done, it doesn't make it right for us to do almost the same thing to him."

"He's getting what he gave to those women, what he almost gave to you. This is justice."

"No, now it's cruel." Ashley watched Nichole crouch beside the man, then look up at Ashley. "Look at him. Look at his aura now."

She looked, not because she was told to, not because she was concerned for the slime that lay sprawled at her feet, but because for the second time that night, she was curious.

What had once been a diseased aura, swimming in colors better suited to an overripe banana, was now pale tan. It seemed as though, by reliving the pain of his victims, he'd redeemed himself. Cleaned his slate.

"You've never seen this before, have you?" Nichole asked.

"No," Ashley admitted. It was the only reply she could give. She'd never bothered to watch the aura of her prey once she cornered them. It served no purpose, or so she'd thought. But now …

The man at her feet had had his soul cleansed, and the idea of taking it now repulsed her. He groaned and mumbled. The word "bitch" was muted, but obvious. He had a chance to better himself, and without realizing it, he would toss it aside.

"He won't change," Ashley said, tilting her head at Nichole.

"But you'll let him live?" She brought her hands together so quickly she almost clapped.

"He won't change, and when he reverts to his old ways the sisterhood will take him."

"He will change for me." Nichole knelt beside the man. He'd loosened sand from the packed earth with his writhing, and now he struggled to lift his face from it.

Irritated with Nichole for being so damn naive and herself for allowing her student to save the man, Ashley stomped back to her car. She retrieved a small knife from under her front seat and walked back to where the other two sat.

Ashley crouched in front of the man and leaned into his face. "Do you remember me?"

His expression scrunched like a baby dirtying his diaper. "I remember." The words seemed a struggle. "Don't like you."

"Good." Her hand grabbed his, prying his palm open and yanking it closer to her. With the tip of the blade she marked his palm, slicing the flesh in a simple pattern.

"This will be your reminder to behave. Every time you look at your hand you will remember how close your sins brought you to death. You've been given a chance to redeem yourself tonight. If you deliberately bring harm to anyone you will be found and what should have happened tonight will happen. Do you understand?" As she asked the question she raised the bloody point of the dagger into the man's face.

"I do, I understand." His eyes crossed, wide with horror as he watched the blade.

Ashley wiped the knife on the hem of her gown. Once a hunter, now he appeared to be a lost child. Although his aura seemed clean Ashley knew it was far from pure.

Nichole placed her hands on the man's face and though she radiated no power her soul seemed to touch his for a moment. "Be good," she whispered to him.

Tears ran down his face as his large hands reached up and covered hers. "I will. Thank you."

The crying gave Ashley pause. She'd seen men cry in agony, in despair, and as a bargaining tool, but never in gratitude.

The man almost skipped to his truck, a beatific smile upon his lips. Nichole seemed exhausted as she walked back to the car, leaving Ashley to stand on the rock-hard earth in the desolate desert. In one naive instant, her world, all of the rules she'd been taught, had just been turned on their ends.

Chapter 7

Ashley's evening wasn't getting better. Nichole rode in the passenger seat in silence for miles, which was fine by Ashley. She'd trained her, nurtured her, and she'd thrown it all away for the slime of humanity.

"Will I be kicked out of the sisterhood?" Nichole asked, echoing Ashley's thoughts.

"I don't know." Best to be honest with her. "I'm not aware of this ever having happened before." *And it happened on my watch.* What would the Mother say? Would she still want her in the inner circle?

She glanced at the woman beside her. Grudging acceptance filled Ashley, drowning out questions of "What was she thinking?" and "How could she do it?" and leaving only "What do we do now?"

"Do you *want* to leave the sisterhood?" Ashley asked the base question she could build upon.

Nichole's reply came immediately. "No, of course not."

"Then you will need to go through with it. You'll need to finish him off."

"I can't."

Ashley gripped the steering wheel in a valiant attempt not to backhand her passenger. "What do you mean you can't? It's not like you went into this with your eyes closed."

"Yes, but in the end, I thought he would still be evil."

"He is," Ashley started to explain.

"He isn't! You felt him, right? You touched his mind after you finished rousing his fear? He wasn't evil anymore. Why don't they train us for that?"

Ashley didn't answer. Of course she hadn't—there was no reason to touch his mind when the only thing left to do was feed. Suddenly, that action felt barbaric. No. Ridiculous. Trying to shake off tendrils of guilt winding their way through her gut, Ashley glared at Nichole.

Her way of life was falling into doubt, and part of her wished they hadn't rescued Nichole. But even as she thought it, she regretted it. All women deserved to be delivered from that hell, no matter how they complicated your life.

"All right, Ms. Angel of Mercy. When he goes after another victim, you'll be there to finish him." She punctuated her statement by poking the dashboard.

Ashley expected silence, but instead the response came quickly. "You removed the evil; he's been punished. He won't return to his old ways."

"It's the nature of men."

"I disagree."

Ashley smacked the steering wheel. "Damn it." They were driving through their neighborhood. "What do we tell the sisterhood? What do we tell the Mother? We couldn't find anyone? You choked? Or that men are inherently good and our business should be to give them a second chance?" She didn't bother to hide the snippiness in her tone.

"I don't know," Nichole whispered. "I'm sorry I've disappointed you."

"Damn." Torn between wanting to comfort the woman beside her and wanting to strangle her, Ashley pulled into the garage, killed the engine, and turned to face her protégé. "Look, since you've been here, you've become a friend. I know for a fact the Mother doesn't induct new sisters easily. When we took you in she read your heart and obviously saw a woman worthy of the sisterhood.

"I'm still that woman."

Ashley took Nichole's pale hand and pattered it. "You've changed, but while we figure out how, and what we are to do about it, we should keep tonight between us."

"Agreed." And with Nichole's nod they went into the house.

Ashley made it to her room without running into anyone; she hoped Nichole did, too. New sisters responded differently to their first successful nights out. Some were exhilarated, needing to recount the tale to everyone who would listen, often several times. Others insisted on being left unaccompanied. So the other sisters would let the successful start the party. Just in case the triumphant sister wished to be alone with her thoughts.

Ashley herself was one of the latter. Stretching out on her bed she lay spread-eagle, a position she'd assumed that evening so long ago, when she'd harvested her first soul. An evening she hadn't thought about for years. She'd insisted on being alone that night.

They'd found him on the street. Stumbling, drunk as a lord, through the streets at twilight. She'd simply walked up to him and reached out to his mind. He'd done so much harm to everyone he knew. He'd beaten his wife and children. He'd stolen from his friends. Initially, she'd been revolted and wanted to jerk away from that horrible mind. But a memory of him pushing his wife down the stairs changed her mind.

She'd made him relive the harm he'd done to his victims over and over until she could remove his soul.

As she sucked, the taste of peaches filled her mouth, rich and sweet. But even as she reveled in the energy that filled her, she saw flashes of other memories. Him being beaten with a belt, being locked in a closet for days, scornful laughter and belittlement. He'd been a victim once.

That gave him no right to inflict it on others.

Her feelings of rage and justice had warred with guilt and shame.

She shook her head. The memories had surfaced quickly, almost consuming her. She forced them back. Locked them down tight.

She changed her position, rolling to her side, and stared out her door.

Nichole lost it in the truck, then. Weak and vulnerable, she must have thought of how her father had been redeemed, which in turn would have brightened her sympathy for the man tonight.

Ashley had seen plenty of that, too. So many women so used to being victims that as soon as the sisterhood dispatched one horrible man the poor woman would shack up with another. Some people didn't have survival instincts.

But then sometimes it took a second chance given by the sisterhood for the women to learn their lesson and make better choices.

Could men be the same? Could they actually choose actions to better themselves?

She stood and paced her small room. Of course they could; self-advancement was foremost on most people's minds, regardless of gender. But could they set aside their own desires for the betterment of others? Could they deny themselves in purely selfless acts?

Nichole surely thought so. They needed to track the hunter's progress. He couldn't be allowed to return to his previous behavior. If necessary, Ashley would finish him herself.

She crossed to her window. The lights of Vegas illuminated the sky. There was still a problem. "With all the people living, working, and playing in this city, how do I pluck a needle out of that haystack?" she asked herself.

"Does one man mean so much?" In the window's reflection, Ashley could see Tarma standing in the doorway.

Thinking quickly, Ashley shrugged. "Another prey we passed over tonight." She didn't move from the sill. "I was wondering if Nichole could find him again."

"Well, that depends … " Tarma's voice and face faded into the background, and another swam into view in the glass: the man with the clean aura. Eric. His curly brown hair framed his unnaturally innocent face. Something about him made her want to be close to him. She wanted to—*Wait. What?*

"What did you say?" Ashley turned.

Tarma sighed. "If she touched his mind she should be able to find him again. Once contact has been made you can recognize their soul."

Ashley considered it for a moment. "Until the other day, when I found prey, I took them. However, sometimes I would have to find out something about him, like where he lived or worked, so I could track him down again." She tapped a fingertip on her chin. "How exactly can I track them by their soul?"

Tarma sat on the edge of Ashley's bed, rekindling memories of Ashley's own training and with them the sense of acceptance and belonging. The sisterhood had made her whole. Damn Nichole.

"Once you've touched their soul, you recognize them the next time you see them. Sometimes, with prolonged exposure—say you were interrupted—you can even track them."

Ashley nodded, but asked, "How?"

"What do you mean 'How'?"

Ashley leaned against the sill. "How can you track them?"

"Souls are exchanged when people are intimate. Touching another's soul is as intimate as you can get."

"So you leave a piece behind?" The idea that all these years she'd shared souls with these slimeballs before doing them in turned her stomach.

Tarma chuckled and jabbed her finger in the air. "That's why we don't tell you while you're in training. Worse than a bug crawling in your ear isn't it?"

Ashley couldn't respond, and when Tarma held out a hand she went and sat beside her, allowing her own mentor to wrap an arm about her shoulders.

"There's nothing to worry about." Tarma gave Ashley a squeeze. "It's a very small piece, and what you give to the men, you get back in the end, understand?"

"Sure, right." She didn't feel better. In fact, it raised other terrible questions. "What if you don't get it back? What does it do to you?"

"If the one you're saving for Nichole doesn't pan out for *her* you should take him." Tarma shrugged. "It's nothing to worry about."

"Right," Ashley said. "Of course. But what if I didn't? What would happen?"

"I don't know, honey. I always go back and get them. It might take a while, but I keep getting drawn back to them, so it's almost irritating. Even if I don't need them, I'll take them because the constant encounters get on my nerves."

That didn't seem so bad. Ashley could handle irritating. "How long have you ever waited?"

"Only one took over a year. I think he was in jail. It took a few years to finally get him. I drove by the compound an inordinate amount of times."

"But it didn't hurt you?"

"No, it's just a little piece." Tarma rose and walked to the door. "Okay now?"

Ashley nodded and shut the door after Tarma left. She still didn't like the idea of that scum running around Las Vegas with a bit of her soul. She'd need to track him down in the morning.

• • •

Ashley went down to breakfast, her mind full and her stomach empty. Even with its persistent growls she wasn't sure if she would be able to keep down the bagel she planned. Too much to consider.

The house wasn't awake yet, though the sun was already high above the horizon. Late to bed, late to rise. Hard to wake with the dawn when sleep comes only three hours before.

As she toasted her bagel, Ashley thought of the man Nichole released. She knew she would need to be the one to track him, as Nichole hadn't touched his soul. And he definitely needed to be tracked.

He was clean for now, but what would become of him later? He could take several victims before being diseased enough to catch the attention of the sisterhood again. Innocent victims who were already piling on her conscience.

On the other hand, what if he had been redeemed? What if they could affect a permanent change on these men? Send them home as the men their abused families hoped they would be?

"Change the world," Ashley whispered to the bagel she pulled from the toaster. It didn't respond, of course, but seconds later, Jamie wandered into the kitchen. She wore her natural look around the mansion.

It was ordinary. Many of the sisterhood had a feature they despised and therefore spent energy to keep it transformed even in private. Jamie had no such flaw. In fact, she had no distinguishing features whatsoever; the memory of her melted away moments after she passed. Before the sisterhood, she had made a comfortable living as a pickpocket.

"Morning," Ashley said, setting out a coffee mug for the bleary-eyed woman.

Jamie jumped. "God. Morning. What are you doing up? I figured you'd have a late night."

"I did." Ashley took a bite of her bagel. Jamie had come into the sisterhood just before Nichole. It was possible all of the others would understand the position Nichole had put Ashley in. However, she decided to keep things to herself for now. All she had was conjecture. She could consider telling the others if Nichole's method was confirmed.

"Didn't go well, huh?" Jamie dug the coffee out of the fridge and started a pot.

"She had different expectations for her prey."

"Not much left of him?" Jamie tapped her nails on the mug she held.

"In a manner of speaking." Ashley took another bite of bagel.

"Always knew that girl would set new standards," Jamie said, pouring more coffee into their mugs.

How could she chat with the others like nothing was wrong? Nichole's experiment had the capability to ruin the sisterhood's existence.

Tarma entered the kitchen, immaculate as always. "Good morning, ladies."

"Morning." Ashley placed the used mug in the dishwasher and moved toward the exit. Tarma would pull the truth from her for sure.

"Wait." The order stopped Ashley in her tracks, so readily did she obey her mentor. "We never talked about how Nichole did last night."

"She's setting new standards," Ashley said, then quickly left the room.

• • •

Morning came too soon for Eric, accompanied by the worst hangover in history. His eyelids felt like sandpaper and his mouth like it had been stuffed with cotton all night. The bedroom was blessedly dark.

For a moment, he lay with his face half buried in his pillow, loath to check the digital clock on his bedside. It was before dawn, this he knew for a fact. He hadn't slept past sunrise since he'd been bitten.

His hangover would be short-lived. As had every injury since he turned. The only good thing to have come from that horrible day.

As he pressed his face into the soft down of the surprisingly comfortable pillow his mind wandered to yesterday's cases. One girl found dead, slightly older than the one taken. One was an orphan, and the other the daughter of a wealthy family. Both were listed as runaways.

"Nothing connects them," he muttered to himself. But Aaron's instinct told him that he was missing something. His subconscious almost had it, but the epiphany slipped away as he woke more.

Grunting in frustration, he turned on the local news. The broadcaster droned on as Eric drank his water and quickly showered. By the time he exited the bathroom to the weather report, his hangover had been washed away.

The weather promised another scorcher. *Astonishing.* As the newscasters started back on the top stories, the mouthful of water Eric had sipped nearly exploded from his lips. A familiar face flashed on the screen.

" … personnel found the man in a hotel room. If you have any information about this man please contact Vegas police." The number flashed under a sketch of the troll from the café the day before. "Police would like to find a person of interest, this woman." There was something familiar about the woman on the screen. He'd never seen her before. However, it was like a tiny voice said, *I know her.*

Chapter 8

Ashley decided she couldn't wait for the hunter to strike again. Men couldn't be trusted even when their own lives were on the line. Following a piece of her soul was harder than Ashley had thought. She felt a general pull to the southwest, but blindly following that pull was impeded by buildings and twisty roads. Occasionally, she was actually driving away from the pull. The effect was dizzying.

She drove with the windows down to let in the morning air. Mornings always held positive meaning for her. As a child, so long ago, she would sneak from the house while her mother and the uncle of the week slept off the night before. The air was fresh and, without the heat and hurt of the coming day, full of potential. But when the adults inside woke up, the magic would break and the day would be ruined.

This early, most tourists would be just getting to bed. Ashley doubted Nichole's experiment was a local. She'd swing by a couple of the off-Strip hotels.

Planning her route, she nearly missed what seemed to be a golden glow coming from the Palace casino up ahead. Odd that this guy was staying in the same hotel as the leprechaun. She pulled into the parking garage and strode though the side door.

Wearing the same guise as the night before, she hoped to instill fear if he recognized her. She didn't worry about the added security at the door. It just confirmed that she wouldn't be able to use the blonde disguise for a while.

Upstairs, she took the elevator to the tenth floor. The closer she came to the little bit of severed soul, the brighter it glowed. Tarma mustn't have been paying close attention if it took her a year to find her prey.

As Ashley approached the door, the glow practically sang to her. It seemed happy. She tried not to think about what could make it change that way. Knocking, she readied herself. If he tried to run she needed to be ready.

The face that greeted her at the door wasn't the hunter, but the guy from the bar, Eric. "What?" she asked before stopping to watch the bit of her soul she'd been tracking bob giddily inside his chest.

"Good morning," Eric said. He didn't seem surprised to see her. "Come in. I just saw you on television."

"What?" she asked again, stepping inside. Did he know? Did he take it on purpose?

"You already said that." The corner of his mouth twitched.

She nearly growled. "Here." It took all of her self-control not to shake him. "What are you doing here?"

"In Vegas?" His face remained stern, but his eyes danced. For all his solemn exterior, he was laughing at her.

"This is your hotel room." Of course he was staying in the city, but how the hell did he get the piece of her that now glowed so happily inside him? *The kiss.* "Who are you?"

"Would you like a drink? I have coffee." He stepped to a table just outside the bathroom and waved at the one-cup coffee maker that sat on top of it.

"Where are you from?"

"Maybe water or tea then?"

"Answer me."

"Have a drink." He patted the mini fridge.

Strangling him wouldn't do. Did he even know what he'd done? She needed to know if there was more of this type of male. Were they organized? "Fine."

The grin he flashed almost outshone the light in his chest.

"Water." She sat on the corner of the bed and waited. He handed her a bottled water and sat on the other corner. Promptly, she moved to the chair of his little desk and faced him. "Now, who are you?"

He didn't say anything until she sipped her water. "As I told you last night, my name is Eric. I'm a private investigator from Chicago. And you are?"

"My name is Ashley. I'm from here." She peered around the room. No sign of the slime that permeated the hunter's aura. In fact, the suite seemed like a typical hotel room: some residue of depravity, but nothing from Eric.

"Excellent," Eric said. "I know as much about you as I did last night." He retrieved a bottle of water for himself and sat again.

"How'd you get it?" she finally asked, deciding to be direct.

"Get what?" His brow creased.

"That piece of me." She stood.

"I didn't ... What?"

"What about your friends?" she demanded. "Did they help you?"

Eric shook his head. "Help me? What are you talking about?" He closed his bottle and set it on the floor beside his feet.

The dancing bit of her soul in his chest got brighter.

"Help you take it." She pointed to his chest.

He glanced at her finger, his eyes wide. "Take what?"

"Me." She felt a tug from the bit of her soul that had snuggled itself into Eric's chest. Then it tugged harder, knocking her off her feet, landing her in Eric's lap.

They both gasped as a second shock wave tore through them. She could smell the coffee on his breath and feel the panting rhythm of his breathing. Her mind went blank. Next thing she knew, she'd grasped his face with both hands and pulled his lips to hers.

She felt the piece in him move. *That's right, come back.* Then another part of her soul made its way out of her body into his. Unlike last night, she felt it happen this time. Panic rose. This wasn't right. She should regain the part she'd lost. She tried to back away, but the two bits joined within him and gripped her closer. Then the hole made by losing a piece of herself was filled with a piece of Eric.

She moaned as the bit slipped into place. She hadn't felt so complete in years, not since she first joined the sisterhood. *Oh, God.*

"I gotta go." Her lips moved against his. She tried to wriggle from his grip.

"Wait," he breathed. His hand caressed her cheek gently. The pressure of his lips against hers softened again. She sank onto his shoulder. The warmth of his arms surrounded her like nothing ever had. She felt secure, wanted, completely safe. Gentle and sweet and deliciously happy.

At that thought, her eyes widened and stared into his. The brown eyes she'd noticed before were filled with flecks of amber. In the center, his pupils dilated, the black void widening. She could get lost in those depths.

The stubble on his face scratched around her mouth, tenderizing her lips with its coarseness. The rough movement sent tingles through her. Closing her eyes, she ran a hand up into the silky curls of his hair.

Too much, too fast. It didn't matter; she didn't want the kiss to end.

A groan escaped her, answered by one from him. She felt his fingers trace the line of her neck. She shifted slightly on his lap. Suddenly, instead of being held, she was being lowered onto the bed.

Whoa. Her eyes flew open. Releasing her grip on him she gasped. "What are you doing?" She stared at him, breathless and panting, hovering over her. She needed him to pause, but she didn't want to stop. A sob almost escaped when he nodded and stood. Running his hands through his hair he backed away from her.

"Sorry," he said, taking a sip of her forgotten water. He shook his head. "I don't know what that was."

Sitting up, she tried to compose herself. The moment was over, and she still had to track down the hunter.

"No problem. I-I should go anyway." She knew what it was. Their souls were mingling. She rolled off the bed, straightened her shirt, and looked to where he stood by one of the large windows.

What had been a happy ball of light now merged with his aura, giving it a two-tone color, white with gold streaks.

Something was happening between them that both frightened and excited her. Did he know? Doubtful. She should tell him, but he probably wouldn't believe her anyway. Right now, she needed to go. Before it got any worse.

She walked to the door, and he followed.

"Will I see you again?" His brow furrowed. He opened his mouth to say something else and closed it. She should tell him something.

"There's something happening between us—" she began.

He stepped closer. Too close. "I've noticed."

Just step out of the door, she told herself. But the piece of him within her kept her frozen in place. "I don't think either of us could prevent it if we tried."

His grin fell. There was so much more to this man than she knew.

Against her better judgment, against all of her training, she reached out to him, the stubble on his chin rough against her fingertips. Then her fingers traced the line of his jaw until they reached the back of his neck. She pulled his mouth to hers.

Again, she felt her soul reach for his. This time, she enjoyed the exchange, almost as much as the dozens of primal sensations that coursed through her that told her to drag him back inside the room and make wild, passionate love to him. The instinct almost got the better of her before she broke the kiss.

"I'll see you again," he whispered. "Soon."

She felt his gaze on her until she turned the corner for the elevator. Unable to help it she smiled all the way back to her car.

•••

Eric closed the door behind Ashley, his mind still reeling from the way she'd grabbed him. That was dangerous. For her as well as him. She wasn't human, she couldn't be. Still, there was something about her. He'd seen, and experienced, too much strangeness since his transformation for this woman to faze him. Something sparked when they were together like with no one he'd ever dated. However …

He had yet to see the real her. What he didn't know about her outnumbered what he did know. She was wanted by the police.

What the hell was happening to them? He'd felt something shift within him when they kissed. Could that be what people meant when they said the earth moved?

•••

Find the hunter. Ashley needed to follow up on Nichole's target from the night before. No matter how often she'd reminded herself of that in the last five minutes, her thoughts returned to Eric.

Just the idea of spending another moment with Eric nearly had her turning the car around.

Nearly.

Nichole's face swam before Ashley's eyes. Tracking the hunter came first. Her poor, innocent protégé who had turned Ashley's world on its ear wasn't cut out to be in the sisterhood. Even if she were right, and men could be permanently redeemed, there was no room for that kind of thinking in the sisterhood. If she were to be honest, many of the sisters enjoyed getting "some of their own back." Until recently, Ashley had felt the same.

Certainly, Ashley didn't need a man. And she didn't want one. Men embraced chaos. They merely used women to satisfy themselves and their needs. Even Eric. There was a shadow in his soul. Something dangerous seemed to lurk just past her reach. She squared her shoulders. He was entertaining, but he should most definitely be avoided.

The hunter is the target. She followed the little tugs like a GPS; the closer she got, the harder they tugged. Ashley pulled into a neighborhood of tract housing. He was local. *Surprising.* The houses looked as though they'd been made with a stucco cookie cutter—small buildings on top of each other with postage-stamp yards.

The street led past rows of homes then around a large circular park and playground area.

Several families picnicked. Hordes of children ran about under the trees and on the jungle gym.

Once upon a time, she'd wanted a family. She slowed the car to watch the interaction at the closest picnic blanket.

A matronly woman watched a young girl of about five run from their blanket to the swings, pigtails flopping as she ran. The child called to be pushed and was answered by the hunter who rose from beside the woman, kissed the hand he held, and walked to the girl.

When he turned to push the child, who now kicked her legs in excitement, Ashley could see the faint piece of her soul in his chest. Still glowing golden and bright.

To get a closer look, she parked her car and walked over to the woman on the blanket. She sat in the grass a few feet from the woman on her right.

After waiting a few moments, Ashley spoke. "Kids are great, aren't they?"

"A blessing," the woman replied without hesitation.

"Your husband looks like a loving father."

"Yes, he does." The awe in the woman's voice spoke volumes, but Ashley chose to err on the side of caution.

"Isn't he?" Ashley asked, hoping to draw her out.

"He's a new man this morning." Then she jumped, as if just realizing she was speaking to a stranger. "He's less stressed today."

Nodding wisely, Ashley said nothing more, but watched the man Nichole had taken mercy on pushing his daughter. None of the vile slime that had so permeated the man's aura the night before remained.

He'd been cleansed. This morning, his entire being reflected a new man. Joyful, spending time with his family.

Ashley looked again at the small bit of her that lived in him. So small, she didn't think she'd miss it. Better to leave it there in case he was to backslide and again become something that needed destroying.

She sighed as she walked back to her car. At least for today the small family could build good memories. Perhaps Nichole was right.

• • •

Ashley returned home to a mansion in turmoil. Tension could be felt from the other side of the front door.

She kept her eyes open for the cause of the cacophony of voices. Nichole sat at the kitchen table, tears streaming down her face. No one else was in sight.

"What's happening?" Ashley asked after she slipped into the kitchen.

"Oh, Ashley," Nichole wailed.

"Shhh," Ashley warned. She didn't know what was going on, and the last thing she wanted to do was get involved in petty sniping. And if it was worse, she wanted to know the situation before she got involved.

"They're sending me away," Nichole gasped through sobs.

"What?" She stood up. "Who? Why?"

"The Mother, because Tarma told her I didn't make the kill last night."

"You told Tarma?" Ashley leaned on the table, struggling with the urge to shake the teary woman. "Why did you do that?"

"I thought if you trusted her I could too," Nichole whispered and looked up at Ashley with big, watery eyes.

Ashley straightened and shoved her fists into the pockets of her jeans. "I told you not to tell anyone. *Anyone*."

"But they should know there's a better way, that we can do our work without killing them." Nichole wiped the tears from her cheeks.

Ashley sighed. "Sure they should, but at what expense?"

"I don't want to leave." Nichole sniffled.

Ashley felt sorry for her. The whole idea that men are able to change was a foreign one to the sisterhood, and it would, of course, be especially difficult for the woman who founded the sisterhood.

"Maybe I could talk to them," Ashley offered.

"Don't, you'll get in trouble too." Nichole blinked her large eyes at Ashley and then they widened larger. "Did you see the guy at the bar again?"

"What do you mean?" Ashley asked, concerned.

"The guy who stole the kiss."

"No," Ashley said, and then remembered seeing her soul in him. If she could see hers in him then others with the power could see his in her. "Shit."

"I can see bits of his soul all over you," Nichole said, standing and hugging the surprised Ashley.

She pressed her hands over her heart. How could she hide this? The sisterhood would kick her out for sure if they caught wind of what she was doing with Eric.

"Oh, God, what do I do?" Ashley pleaded of the air.

"Why don't you concentrate your power on your aura? Instead of disguising your physical appearance, alter your own aura?"

"It could work." Ashley concentrated on herself and her own aura. The effort had perspiration beading across her forehead.

Finally, after quite a bit of pushing, Nichole told her she had it. Just in time, because a second later, Tarma walked into the room.

"Ashley?" The question sounded like a whip in the silence. Ashley spun to face her mentor.

"Yes?" Ashley smiled and gulped down the sudden string of excuses that rose in her throat. She had nothing to explain.

"You left the house early this morning. I needed to talk to you."

"Sure, I—"

"The Mother wanted to talk to you." Tarma stared at Ashley, her eyes flickering as if she meant to see through her.

Confidence, Ashley reminded herself. "Sure. Is she here now?"

"Yes." Tarma led the way up the stairs.

"What did you need to talk to me about?" Ashley asked, focusing on the paintings along the stairs and hall.

She'd seen them before, heck, she'd lived in this house and walked these halls for years. But today, they took on a whole new meaning for her.

Just at the top of the stairs hung an angry abstract of reds, oranges, and blacks that seemed to flicker in the light of the stairwell. She could swear she felt heat emanating from it.

Farther along the hallway, another looked like a portrait of a marriage kiss in an outdoor wedding, but as she passed, the bride appeared to be eating the groom. Ashley choked back her exclamation and was overcome with a bout of coughing. Why hadn't she seen any of these things before?

"You understand Nichole will have to leave?" Tarma asked, pausing before another flight of stairs.

"Of course." Ashley met her old mentor's eyes. For the first time, she saw the vertical slits where her pupils should have been. "She doesn't belong here." Ashley didn't think she would be able to lie, so she stayed with the truth.

"She seems to believe men are worth saving, able to be reformed." Tarma let the statement hang between them, heavy with the implied question: did Ashley believe the same thing?

Ashley responded as she would have three days ago. "I'm sorry she'll have to leave. She had promise."

Again, Tarma waited. The silence, though obviously for effect, nearly unnerved Ashley.

Finally, after twenty seconds that seemed to last twenty minutes, they continued up the stairs. The heavy wooden doors to the Mother's bedroom opened by themselves as Tarma approached.

"Ah, it's about time, Ashley." The Mother walked to the door, clasped Tarma's hands, and then turned to Ashley. "I'm glad we caught you before you went hunting this evening." She led Ashley by the hand to an antique couch by the open French doors that overlooked the garden with a view of the desert beyond.

Ashley'd been in this room on several occasions, and never before had she had the overwhelming dread that she had now.

A light dry breeze blew through the doorway. It was warm and pleasant, but it chilled her to the bone.

"You've had a lot to deal with, dear." The tone was strong and sweet. Ashley wanted to believe the kindness in her words as she'd done so many times before, but her mind picked apart every word, looking for an inner meaning.

"You look a little dehydrated." The Mother passed her a glass. "Have a drink."

Ashley thanked her and sipped. But the Mother placed a finger under the glass and lifted the bottom. "Drink up. We don't want your promotion to suffer because you're not caring for yourself properly."

The drink seemed fizzy like peroxide, but it tasted like cinnamon. She finished the glass, and before she could inspect the empty vessel the Mother handed it to Tarma and continued, "Nichole wasn't ready to join the sisterhood. I saw potential in her, but she proved that she just doesn't have what it takes." All Ashley could do was nod, as the bony hand patted hers. "You mustn't blame yourself for her failure. She had radical ideas unworthy of a member of the sisterhood."

The skeletal fingers dug into the back of Ashley's hand. She held in a gasp and endured the pain. "You're not placing any stock in those ideas, are you, dear?"

Ashley replied quickly, knowing any hesitation could be used against her. "I told her the idea was ridiculous at the start."

"Good. That's good." The vise released, and Ashley's battered hand received another pat. "This will allow you the opportunity to deal with an unfit sister. It is not part of your training, but I see how valuable it will be to you."

"Okay."

Tarma circled to stand just behind Ashley. The Mother seemed not to notice. "Of course, she knows too much to set her loose into the world. We can't guarantee her silence out there, so she'll have to be dealt with by us. Well, by you."

"Dealt with?"

"Your very first." The Mother patted her hand again; she seemed proud.

Tarma, on the other hand, rolled her eyes. "Sentimentality is a weakness." It wasn't imagined; she hissed like a lizard.

"Tarma's right. It can be." The Mother narrowed her eyes at the hovering woman. "However, tonight, we celebrate."

A celebration. Dealt with.

Tarma gripped Ashley's shoulders and squeezed. "If you drain her quickly it won't bother you as much. Do you feel it inside you yet?"

Ashley fought to keep her facial muscles relaxed. They wanted her to kill Nichole. Could she even do that? At one time, maybe, but now … Ashley's stomach clenched, and she swam through a wave of nausea. What had they put inside her? The way they talked it was more than energy, more than a spirit.

"You and Tarma should hunt together for a while. She will be able to teach you some new techniques. Help you embrace the spirit within you."

"That's great. I've missed hunting with her." Ashley smiled, but her vision blurred for a second as she gazed at both of the other women. But they weren't women. They were powerful creatures that for the first time she could see clearly.

The Mother looked the most familiar. Then, Ashley realized the tapestry over the large bed was a portrait. Scales as black as coal. Eyes that defied nature by being even darker.

Tarma looked similar to the Mother, except instead of being shiny, coal-black, her skin was a deep, forest green. Both of their auras were tinged with the blood of a recent kill.

No hesitation, absolutely no revulsion, Ashley thought. She couldn't let them see what she really thought, the fear she felt. The part of Eric inside her warmed, giving her strength.

"It's been a while since I've hunted with someone that knows what she's doing," Ashley added as she leaned back a little and crossed her legs.

"Good. Then it's settled." The Mother stood and clasped both of Ashley's hands, pulling her up with her. "Now, go fetch Nichole so we can get this unhappy part over with." Then she released her.

At her cue, Ashley left the room.

The door had almost closed when she felt it being pulled back and open again. She glanced back, and what she saw caused her to lose her grip on the knob. Talons extended from the green scaled fingers that curled around the door from the inside.

Once Ashley stepped away from the door, the hand returned to the well-manicured appendage of her mentor. The seconds between releasing the door and seeing Tarma's face were barely enough for Ashley to regain her composure.

"Ashley." The woman's smile chilled her as it never had before. "Would you mind telling Jessie to pick up some ice cream on her way home this evening?"

"Sure." Ashley didn't run but walked briskly to her bedroom. A quick scan told her there was nothing of value to salvage. Slipping a purse over her shoulder, she left.

The Mother was right about one thing: Nichole didn't belong in the sisterhood. Now Ashley realized that she didn't either. She swallowed and prepared to leave her home of forty years.

If either of those creatures caught wind of her connection to Eric, he would be in danger, too.

Chapter 9

Ashley barely controlled her descent of the stairs. Running wouldn't do, not if she were going to get Nichole. When she peeked into the front sitting room she found Nichole, hands folded, waiting.

Ashley tapped her shoulder and forced a smile. "Let's go to lunch."

"Ooh, that sounds lovely. But Tarma told me to wait." Her shoulders slumped slightly. "They're probably going to wipe my memory."

She couldn't let her anxiety show, and there was no way she could explain. "Before you forget me entirely would you mind if we had one last lunch first?"

The corners of Nichole's lips quirked slightly.

"I know." She reached for Nichole's shoulder and steered her to the front door. "I'll get it out of my system at lunch."

Calmly, they walked to one of the sisterhood's cars. She dare not run, though she had no idea what would happen if they were caught. She had a feeling that a last lunch wouldn't fly with Tarma and the Mother.

When they were on the road, Nichole asked, "Where are we going for lunch?"

"Nowhere." A side glance revealed a pout. "I had to get you out of there. I couldn't take you upstairs."

"Why? They were just going to erase my memory."

"No, they weren't." Ashley had no idea where she intended to drive. Silence.

"They want you dead," Ashley said, pulling onto the freeway. Nichole needed to know the truth.

"Nonsense. I'm not a man. I'm one of the sisterhood, and a woman."

"You're not a member until your induction ceremony and as far as being a woman goes, I don't think that matters anymore." *If it ever did.* "They ordered me to kill you."

Nichole exhaled slowly.

"Don't worry, I won't."

Nichole's eyes widened slightly, and she patted Ashley's leg. "I know you'd never hurt me. Where are we going?"

Ashley bit her tongue. Had this situation arisen just a couple of days ago she very well might have served Nichole's soul to the Mother on a silver platter.

"I haven't a clue," Ashley admitted. Even before she knew something sinister lay beneath the surface of Tarma and the Mother, she wouldn't have thought it possible to run from the sisterhood. Now it was the only way she could see a future, for her or Nichole.

Chapter 10

Eric worked to put Ashley's morning visit aside. Aaron had agreed to let him review the original file of the murdered girl, Suzie Hogan. Even as he read the details of the case, Ashley came into his mind unbidden. Repeatedly, he pushed her image aside to focus on the folder in front of him. There would be plenty of time to work out the mysteries of that woman later.

The poor girl's end began as a kidnapping.

Before Suzie's disappearance, she lived at the Angola Center for Displaced Girls. According to the report, the last any adult saw of her was on her way to the school bus stop. No children were interviewed.

The report was functionary, written by an overworked individual and dictated by a similar person, both of whom most likely saw too many runaways to think anything strange in yet another young woman who decided life would be better on her own.

He needed to re-interview the staff at the center and the girl's friends.

He made a quick call to Max, who agreed to play chauffeur and access card. With a single flash of Max's badge the two of them were escorted through the hallways to the principal's office. The walls were yellowed to the point of almost being brown around the corners and moldings. It reminded Eric of his neighbor's house growing up. His friend's parents smoked, and the tobacco stained everything. When they moved out, there were squares of blue on the green walls where the pictures had been removed. Time had its own color palette.

He could hear the murmur of voices as he and Max moved deeper into the building, and picked up the scent of stale coffee, pancakes, and maple syrup. Not the homiest place to grow up, but it beat living on the street. It was probably better than skipping around foster homes. His old partner would know.

They followed the elderly receptionist through a pair of glass French doors at the end of the yellow hall and entered the principal's office. A sign beside the doors labeled it as belonging to *Dr. Lucy Callie, Principal*. Behind the heavy wooden desk sat a woman with tired eyes but a quick smile. "What can I do for you, Officer?"

Max shook her extended hand. "My associate, Detective Adams, has a couple questions for you regarding Suzie Hogan."

Principal Callie tapped on her computer's keyboard. "She's one of our girls?"

"No, ma'am, at least not currently," Max responded.

She abandoned her computer and tilted her head.

"Six months ago you had a runaway named Suzie Hogan," Eric explained.

Now the rest of her face matched her eyes. "Unfortunately, we have a lot of girls come through here and far too many runaways. It's difficult to remember them all."

Eric held out a copy of the missing person's report; the girl's picture had been stapled in the top corner.

"Yes, I remember her. She wasn't very happy here. Many of the girls aren't. She talked about making her way to California to become an actress. I figured that's where she went."

"Do you have any of her belongings that weren't stored with the missing person's file?"

"No, but sometimes before the runaways leave, they pass on a belonging or two to their friends. You can talk to her roommates."

"Could we see her room as well, please?"

Her brow furrowed a moment. "Of course."

Eric nodded. It was possible that the girl's belongings could harbor the scent of her abductor. Hopefully another clue would follow.

...

Instinct had Ashley driving through the city. She had no real direction but she knew she needed to hide Nichole in a place that the sisterhood normally wouldn't go. Finally, she saw a light that called her like a beacon. Then she felt a pleasant tug. She pulled into the parking lot of what appeared to be a school. She parked directly behind a marked police car. Close to even inept police would still be safer than in the middle of nowhere.

"I know this place," Nichole said. "I was sent to live here after my parents died."

Perhaps Nichole would be safe here. At least for a while. "Maybe they have a position available. Didn't you used to be a cook?"

Nichole nodded. They entered the building and followed the long hallway. A few steps from the closed office door, Ashley wondered at the wisdom of seeking his company. "Maybe we should go."

The door opened. Voices crept through before anyone was visible.

A squeal of delight sounded from Nichole just before she launched herself at the woman who stepped through the door. The woman endured the hug with a smile and patted Nichole's blonde hair. "Dr. Callie." Nichole squealed again.

Eric's gaze met Ashley's. It felt like he almost smiled, though his expression remained stern. She'd resumed the form similar to the one she usually took, a heart-shaped face and blue eyes with golden blonde hair. He'd never seen this form before, but he knew her. She could tell that somehow he could see through her disguises.

Once she had the excited woman at arm's length, Dr. Callie recognized her former resident. "Nichole Braden. How are you? What brings you back here?" The old woman's tired face came to life.

"Looking for a job," Ashley answered, gripping Nichole's arm to silence her.

"I might have something available." Dr. Callie glanced at Ashley and returned her attention to Nichole. "I have to take these gentlemen to room 235." She seemed distracted and much more interested in talking with Nichole than with anything the "gentlemen" were doing. "They are investigating a young woman who ran away. I have to show them to her former room." She linked an arm through Nichole's. "Walk with me and tell me what you are up to these days."

"Well, for one thing, Tarma got really mad at me."

"Who's Tarma?"

Ashley wanted to strangle Nichole. "Her boss. That's why she needs work."

They started up the stairs with Dr. Callie asking about Nichole's work experience. By now, Nichole had fortunately begun to catch on to watching what she said. So Ashley hung back and tried not to focus on the quizzical glances Eric sent her.

The officer with him had been with him at the bar, too. Luckily, he didn't notice anything out of the ordinary. He simply smiled and nodded. By the time they'd arrived at the room, Dr. Callie had found a position for Nichole working in the kitchen at the center.

"All of the beds in this room are occupied. I'm not sure what you think you'll be able to find. The girls who don't have classes this hour are in the library, so you have time to look around," Dr. Callie said. "Take as many pictures as you need, just please put everything back where you found it. The young ladies can be very particular about who touches their belongings." To Nichole, she said, "Let's go down to my office and get the forms."

Nichole slipped the onyx band from her finger and pressed it into Ashley's hand. As she walked away she twiddled her bare fingers at her former mentor.

The officer turned toward the open door then, as if having just noticed that she still stood there. "Can we help you, miss?" he asked.

She didn't know how to respond. She just looked at Eric.

To Max, he said, "She's a friend." To her, he said, "I need to take care of this right now. Will you wait here?"

She could only nod and lean against the hallway wall. They needed to talk. He had an idea of how she kept finding him, but this time he deserved an explanation or at least the semblance of one. She tapped a light rhythm on the wall behind her. That sort of conversation could get messy.

. . .

Eric forced his attention to the investigation. There would be time enough to deal with the woman waiting for him in the hallway later.

Suzie used to live with two other girls. They each had a bed and a desk. Their dresser drawers were built into the bed frame under the mattress. Each bed had been neatly made, and there wasn't a scrap of clothing on the floor. There must be rules against leaving an untidy area. From what Eric remembered of his own adolescence, most children weren't neat unless coerced.

Starting with the things to the right of the door, Eric opened the drawers of the desk just long enough for a sniff and then closed it.

Max watched for a second and then cleared his throat. "You seem to have a method."

Moving to the drawers under the bed, Eric said, "Yup."

Max rocked to his toes and back again. "I'll just take a peek in the closet."

"Fine."

His nose told him the floor was mopped and the bedding changed regularly. One girl had a stash of candy bars in the back of her desk. Another had a stash of pot under her mattress. He'd cleared most of the room when, finally, his nose caught a scent. He crossed the room to the closet and leaned against the frame. He asked, "Find anything?" before taking a whiff.

Nothing.

As if confirming Eric's perception, Max grunted. "Nothing. Lots of shoes, just nothing useful."

The smell came from somewhere. He made to move back to where he'd left off and smelled it again. There, on the bed—under the covers—no—in a cigar box, tucked between the wall and the mattress. A rag doll in what appeared to be jeans and a black t-shirt.

"Bingo." He could smell the killer—faint, but there. Now if only there were a national scent registry, they'd be golden.

Max stood from where he was replacing shoeboxes. "That looks familiar." He dug gloves and an evidence bag from his pocket.

"Suzie didn't run away," Eric said, holding the pillow up so Max could remove the doll.

"But if she was abducted it was off the street. How did the doll get here?" Max placed the doll in the evidence bag and sealed it. Then he tucked his gloves back into his pocket.

"Let's ask Dr. Callie. We'll need to interview the occupant of this bed."

As they left the room Eric told Max to go on ahead so he could hang back to talk to the gorgeous honeyed blonde who still waited for him in the hall.

"One of these days I'm going to need to know what you really look like." He tucked his hands into his pockets.

"We need to talk."

"Yes." He used to go for this type. Blonde and curvy. But more than her looks, which seemed to change from one hour to the next, her scent drove him wild. Floral and woody. Rich and scintillating. "Do you have a car?"

Her eyes widened, and she shook her head. "Yes, but—"

He continued without giving her a chance to tell him why it wouldn't work out. "I have a few more things to do here. If you could wait for me, I'll treat you to lunch."

"I—we—" she floundered.

"Good."

He descended the staircase quickly. She was the one that kept finding him. She was the one that first said they needed to talk. She could wait.

Dr. Callie was already talking to Max when Eric entered the room. "Rachael brought it back from school one day. She said something about it being what Suzie left behind. I thought it was something Suzie gave to Rachael when she decided to leave."

"Had you ever seen *Suzie* with the doll before?" Eric asked.

"I don't think so. Honestly, I didn't think anything of it."

"We know," Max said as he tapped the end of his pen against his jaw. "Is there a way you could call Rachael in here so we can ask her a few questions?"

"I'll need to be present during questioning," Dr. Callie said as she dialed an extension.

"Of course." Max notated that Dr. Callie would serve as Rachael's *guardian ad litem*.

Within minutes, a young lady about fifteen entered Dr. Callie's office and sat. Her blonde hair was pulled back in a ponytail that reached her shoulders. Wisps of stray hair had pulled free and wandered across her face. Saucers of blue stared at the three adults and waited. This young lady knew from a young age to only answer the most direct questions.

Max took the lead. Pulling the bagged doll from his pocket he placed it on the desk in front of the girl. She reached a hand toward it, then thought twice, and clasped her hands together on her lap. "What can you tell me about this doll?" Max asked.

"It's mine," she said, her fingers flexed.

"Where did you get it?" he asked, keeping his voice light.

"Suzie left it for me."

"How do you know that?"

"Because it was dressed just like her, and she left it in our spot."

"Your spot?"

"You know, where we stood while we waited for the bus." Everyone nodded. "I stopped to talk to Mickey Marino." She glanced at Dr. Callie. "He's really nice, but he was out of school 'cause of the flu or something so he was asking me about homework."

Dr. Callie nodded and motioned for the girl to continue.

"Suzie said she would meet me at our spot. Mickey and I walked slow 'cause I was showing him something in the book or something and when we turned the corner, she wasn't there. I thought she might have sat back in the bushes. We did that sometimes, too. Ya know, out of the sun. She wasn't back there, but this doll was. It was dressed just like her. She was always talking about running away to Hollywood. She kept saying about how it was so close and all she had to do was hitch a ride. I figured she stopped talking about it and just decided to go."

"Without saying goodbye to her best friend?" Eric asked.

"That's what the doll was, her way of saying goodbye." Again, she reached for it and stopped herself. "Why is it in the bag? Can I have it back?"

The doll was six months old. The scent of the kidnapper was there, but to anyone else it was doubtful there would be anything of use there at all. And Rachael believed it was the only thing she had of her lost friend.

"We have to keep it for just a little while. But when we are done we'll make sure you get it back," Eric said.

"Soon?" she asked.

Max crouched beside the girl's chair. "It may take a while. But as soon as we can."

She crossed her arms. "Don't forget."

"I'll bet Dr. Callie will make sure we don't forget," Eric said, winking at Rachael.

The girl sat straighter now and smiled so the stray lock of hair swung away from her face. "Oh, no. She remembers everything."

The principal smiled. "I'll make sure to keep checking with them until they are done with it."

Max stood, and both men shook Dr. Callie's hand. "I think we have all we need. My number is on the receipt for the doll."

They exited the building.

"So, he's not *just* a kidnapper," Eric murmured. The feds would be involved for sure. They were always notified for missing children but didn't always take an active role. Now that the kidnapper had graduated to murderer, they would be all over this. Eric would have to function in front of them. Explain himself. His stomach knotted.

"I'll take this to the lab and see what they can get off of it after all this time." Max cleared his throat and opened his car door. "You go ahead and take care of your business."

Eric had been following Max to his car without thinking. But when the officer cleared his throat Eric looked up to see Ashley leaning against her SUV, watching him. "Right," he said to Max and simply stood still till the officer drove away, leaving him alone with Ashley.

"Where do you want to go for lunch?" she asked.

His mind, still concerned with the upcoming federal investigation, didn't quite register what she said. "What?"

"Food." She spoke slowly. "Eat. Talk. You buy."

That's right. "Our third date. We could always go back to my hotel and order room service." The flirtation came unbidden. If she took him up on it what else might he do without thinking? Still, the entertainment of verbally fencing with this enigma of a woman began to ease the queasiness.

She grunted. "A restaurant." A smile played at the corners of her mouth. "I'll pick."

Chapter 11

Sitar music and the unmistakable scent of curry spiced the air. Once they were seated in the dimly lit Indian restaurant decorated in dark maroon and gold she began to relax somewhat. A small buffet had been set up in the corner near the kitchen, but Ashley had ordered for them.

From her studies of the sisterhood's library over the years she knew the symbols on each table were meant to encourage harmony. She also knew the symbols over the door were an ancient spell to keep away evil spirits. The sisterhood learned these so they wouldn't hunt in places with these marks. They said it was because there was no prey, but now she wasn't so sure. She had no idea what would happen if she did, but she knew no one from the sisterhood would attempt to follow her here.

Eric hadn't seemed himself when he came out of the center. But as they drove, he seemed to shake off the burden that weighed on him. Now, as he sat across from her, he cocked his head and smiled. "Did you want to start the conversation? You're the one who said we needed to talk."

"You know I'm not who I appear to be." She hesitated; how could you tell someone that fairy tales are true? That not everyone is human?

"I can tell that you're you no matter whose face you wear." He sipped his water.

"You know I can—?" She fell silent as the waiter delivered their food.

Coconut curry lamb and what Ashley only knew as butter chicken. Next came a big bowl of jasmine rice and a plate of naan bread. The waiter refilled their water and then took a closer look at Eric.

Realizing he was the subject of scrutiny, Eric smiled at the waiter. The man whispered something in another language and leaned closer. They were nearly ear to ear before Eric's eyebrows rose and he leaned back. Now it was the waiter's turn to smile. He placed a card on the table next to Eric's plate. To Ashley, he nodded. "Please enjoy."

Eric tucked the card in his pocket, glancing over his shoulder at the retreating waiter, and chuckled. When he caught Ashley's gaze, he shrugged. "Extremely distant relation."

He scooped food from the plates in the center of the table onto his own and tasted. "This is very good. I haven't tried Indian food before. I like it."

She watched him eat, then served herself. She really hadn't thought this through. The place was safe enough, but there were people around. The entire staff of the restaurant seemed to be taking turns gazing their way. For some reason, they'd become far less anonymous. Anyone could overhear. "Perhaps we *should* talk somewhere more private."

He grunted. "I'm comfortable here, but if you need somewhere private there's always my hotel room."

"That sounds good."

That broke his concentration on his food. "Really?"

Why did he sound nervous? "Don't worry, we can finish lunch first," she teased.

He watched her for a moment. She tried to eat without self-consciousness, and failed. When she returned his gaze, he asked, "Who was the girl with you earlier?"

Lucky for her, she'd been thinking about how to describe the situation in real-world vernacular since she first ran into him that afternoon. "Something of a coworker. A trainee. Turns out she isn't really right for the job. Got into some trouble with our boss and was about to be fired. It seems as though she'll be able to get a fresh start at the center."

"Good. Where do you work?" he asked.

"That's a subject better left for later." She spooned a little more rice onto her plate.

"How long have you worked there?"

"Yeah, that should wait for later, too." She dipped a piece of naan into the sauce on her plate and bit into it.

"Is there anything you can tell me that doesn't have to wait till later? Family? Hobbies?"

She thought a moment. She had no other family besides the sisterhood. Now she didn't even have that. Her own parents died early, though she would have outlived them anyway. Images of her childhood seemed to waft from some ethereal plane. She and her mother wearing aprons and carefully pouring something into a pan. Laughter like angels singing. Sweet bread fresh from the oven smeared with jam they'd put away the year before.

Tears welled. She hadn't thought of her mother in decades. "Baking." She sniffed. "I like to bake."

"It doesn't look like you like it."

"My mother and I used to bake together before she died."

"I'm sorry for your loss." He reached for her hand.

"It was a long time ago." She dabbed at her eyes and sipped her water. "I guess I've been too focused at work to think about much else. I haven't baked since she died. I do read a lot, though."

"I like to read almost everything. I've even read a romance or two. What do you like to read?"

"Cookbooks. Nonfiction … " *Mostly stuff in the sisterhood library.* Now that she thought about it, she realized that it was mostly feminist occult type stuff. She coughed.

"No, that's okay." He cleared his throat. "It looks like I've eaten the lion's share. Go ahead and finish yours. I'll be right back."

He crossed to the register and paid for their meal, then was engaged in conversation by their waiter. The two of them were quickly surrounded, and the manager herded the chattering group into another room.

Leaving the table while your lunch companion was still eating was rude. It wasn't his fault—he'd only gone to pay, she reminded herself. The waiter had somehow discovered they were related. They must be catching up. But … Eric didn't look Indian. She'd just finished eating when Eric returned.

"Planning a family reunion?" she asked.

"Something like that." He extended a hand. "Ready to go back to my place?" He waggled his eyebrows in outrageous suggestion.

• • •

On the drive over, she changed her look again. It was thrilling to watch her transform. It took some concentration to refrain from touching her arm as her tone darkened. Now she had dark-chocolate skin and a very revealing white sundress. The contrast was appealing. The fact that it was still her made it tantalizing.

He opened the door to his hotel room for her, and when he closed it, she slid the privacy lock closed.

"So … " He raked his eyes over her ebony body. "Are you a natural brunette?"

"Why doesn't this freak you out?" She seemed irritated at his easy acceptance. Of course, that made it more fun to bother her. "What's your deal?"

He pulled two bottled waters from the mini fridge, passed her one, and took a sip of his own. "You first."

She squared her shoulders. "I'm a member of the sisterhood."

He shrugged. "I'm a member of Marroni's Gym."

They stared at each other for a while. He could see very clearly she was fighting the urge to smack him. He let the corner of his mouth rise a bit. "Okay, what is the sisterhood?"

"It is a group of women. Their main goal is to rid the world of men's evil."

"I take it you don't mean mankind's evil." He sipped his water and sat on the edge of the bed.

She shook her head.

"And how do they do the ridding?"

"By removing their souls and thereby their lives."

His small smile was gone now. He'd heard about them before. Back home, a drug dealer had run into the precinct naked and raving about sisters who wanted to eat his soul, but Eric hadn't believed they existed. But then *he* existed, so why shouldn't they? "You're a succubus."

This time, it was she who shrugged. "I never thought of myself like that. I suppose I am. I wasn't born this way."

He nodded and closed the cap on this water bottle. "I was reborn last year." It was still hard to admit it. Even having beaten the curse, and with all the good that it had allowed him to do, he still felt ... Was it shame? He forced out the words. "As a werewolf."

Ashley stepped back.

"No need to fear. The curse is beatable. I mean, I'm still a werewolf, but it doesn't control me." Eric's shoulders sagged. "Physically, at least," he whispered. The conversation wasn't going well. He hadn't planned on sharing that with her, and now she was afraid. He took a deep breath and focused on the positive. She hadn't run yet.

"Yeah, but it's ... " Her eyes darted about as she searched for the right word. "Contagious."

"I don't bite." He rubbed a hand across his face. "I've never talked about this with a non-werewolf before." Her doubt resonated from her as she maintained her distance. "No, really, the one that made me was a serial killer. He used me as bait to get to my partner. She killed him. Then she and her husband helped me beat the curse, kept me from killing during my first full moon, but ... "

It hurt for him to admit what he had become. He was strong, though, strong enough to keep going. Strong enough not to turn the hurt onto someone else.

* * *

She had hurt like that so many years ago. Then Tarma came and helped her out of the abyss. If only she could do that for Eric now. Every part of her wanted to try. No matter what he felt about what he'd become, he wasn't the monster he thought he was.

She'd never known a werewolf before, but she supposed if succubae could exist, so could werewolves. Now she knew how he knew her when she shifted. She must smell the same. The small spark of delight at figuring out the puzzle dimmed with his pain.

She reached for him and took his hand. Then she scooted closer. She could already sense his wariness of her next move. Sliding still closer, she leaned into his neck and inhaled the combination of shampoo, cologne, and man. She sighed.

His trembling fingers traced their way up her thigh, and she shivered in anticipation.

His breathing deepened and then stopped.

She leaned back. His eyes were squeezed shut, and his lips pressed together into a thin line. Why did he stop himself? He wasn't repulsed by her ... or was he? "What is it?"

She pulled away further, but his hand caught hers before she could leave his side completely. "I can't be cavalier about this. There was a time—" He shook his head. His eyes pleaded with her to understand. "Even once for me now means forever. I ... we need to be sure."

"Sure of us?" She chuckled softly. "I'm not even sure of me anymore. A week ago I would have separated your soul from your body without a moment of hesitation. I was always taught that if I hesitated—heck, if any woman hesitates—to see if a man is more than he seems, I put the world in danger.

"But I let you in. Because of Nichole, I hesitated with you and not only are you more than you seemed, you're doing something to me." She squeezed his fingers. "But you need to know, I am sure of you. I can see your soul, even if you can't. You are not a monster.

"I was married when I was barely a woman; the sisterhood saved me shortly after. I lived with them for four decades."

His eyebrows rose as he did the math.

"Eric, I haven't even attempted to love someone for forty years. I don't know that I've ever made love. If you must wait, I can do that." She winked. "When you reach my age you get good at waiting."

That got a chuckle from him. She could see his pain ease.

Together, they lay back on the bed, fingers entwined. He cleared his throat. "You are a succubus." When she nodded, he continued, "You were training the other woman, Nichole. Why?"

"I was going to be a part of the inner circle." She'd been so proud; now the thought sent a wave of disgust through her.

He grunted. "A promotion. You must have been good at your job."

"Yes."

"What does that entail? You wouldn't get a raise?"

"I didn't know at first. After I pledged to train Nichole, I was taken for a ceremony to take in the spirit. I wonder now if that meant something more. It's possible they are trying to make me into a demon."

"Sounds like fun." He stiffened a little, but he didn't release her hand.

"I might have gone along with it, until I met Nichole." It felt important for her to admit it to him.

"Oh." His thumb stroked hers.

"She had some crazy idea that men could be redeemed."

"Absolutely insane." Not a hint of sarcasm tinted his words.

"It was. But the other night—the night you and I first spoke, in fact—she stopped me short of ripping a man's soul out completely. I was so close. But she saved him. When I tracked him down later his wife said he was a new man. He seemed like it. He seemed fulfilled. It's like I gave him a second chance at making the right choice."

"That sounds great. What's the problem?" He nudged her foot with his toe.

"I think the Mother, our leader, already knew about the ability to give second chances. I don't think she cares. Nichole told them about her ideas, and they asked me to take care of her."

"They asked you to kill her. Your own student."

"Yes. They told me to do it quick so it wouldn't bother me so much. Now I've helped her escape, and they'll know that I know their secret. They'll be after me next. All they would have to do is extract her soul to learn everything that's happened. Then they would know about me. About us. We haven't gone too far for you, but we've already crossed the point of no return for me."

She withdrew her hand from his and propped herself up on one elbow to face him. "You want to know how I keep finding you? Our souls have begun to mingle. You carry pieces of me in you." She placed a finger on his chest. "I couldn't release the pieces of you if I tried, and for a while, I did try. I can see the bits of me are happy here." She tapped him again. "I wouldn't want to move them now if I could. If the sisterhood finds out any of this they will destroy us both."

She rested her forehead against his solid chest, exhausted. Emotionally drained. She wanted to be with this man every waking moment of the day. But if anyone found out, the two of them would be eradicated. Their souls fed to demons only the Mother knew.

Love had made her miserable, just as the sisterhood had promised it would.

...

Screams pierced the darkness. Deep throaty shrieks and heavy flapping wings of a demon on the attack echoed in stark contrast to the high-pitched wails of a woman in pain. The musky scent of scales swept away by the breeze.

"Ashley. Help me." Nichole gasped before the creature dove again, talons outstretched.

...

"Nichole." Ashley woke from where she'd been snuggled against Eric. They'd fallen asleep clothed. She got out of bed and checked her pocket for her keys.

He'd opened his eyes when she sat up in bed; now he was standing too. "What's wrong?"

"I think they found her." She found her keys. "I have to go to the center."

"You're not going alone." He slipped on a holster and gun, then his leather jacket on top of that.

They raced to the parking garage. At one in the morning, the party scene in Vegas was starting to get really hot. The press of cars on the Strip made Ashley wish jumping out and running could get her there faster.

Finally, traffic started to move. Once they were clear of the Strip, Eric asked, "How do you know she's in trouble?"

"She called out to me."

"Succubae are telepathic?"

"We're connected. You wouldn't understand." She raced through a yellow light.

"Careful, a speeding ticket will only slow us down."

She decelerated a little. Almost there. They flew around a corner and nearly into a limo with six women sticking their heads out of the moon roof. The sound of Nichole's screams seemed to echo in her ears. Ashley skidded into the parking lot sideways, finally coming to a stop so close to the side of the center's van she had to crawl out of Eric's door.

There was no sound besides their labored breathing.

"Where is she?" Ashley demanded.

There was no bellow of demons or flapping of wings. Only traffic in the distance.

She ran to the center's front doors and then around the side of the building to look into their field area. "Where is she?"

Eric had drawn his weapon when he got out of the car. But as they stood in the quiet parking lot, no evidence of any activity around the building, he put it away. "Ashley, there's no one here."

She stood staring at the building. "There has to be."

"The only people are inside. Asleep." He crossed to her and wrapped his arms around her. "Could it have just been a nightmare?"

"No." She looked around again. "It was so real."

"We can come back in the morning to talk to her if you want."

"Yeah." She nodded slowly, sorting through the images in her dream. What had she seen? Nichole, broken and bleeding. Collapsed on asphalt. It was a parking lot. Dark asphalt and bright yellow lines. Ashley looked at her feet as Eric led her to the car. The lot was faded to a light gray even in the dim light. The lines of the spaces were pale white.

"It wasn't this parking lot." Ashley jerked her shoulder away from Eric. "Either Nichole wasn't attacked here—"

"Then where would she be?"

"Right, or—"

A flap of wings overhead revealed the answer. "It was a trap," Eric finished, drawing his gun again.

Doors slammed. Nichole called from the door of the center. "Ashley!"

"It still is," Eric yelled as he grabbed her arm and propelled her toward the front doors. A deep musk descended, covering them like a blanket. The deep sound of flapping wings circled overhead, out of sight, but every beat an ominous rhythm. With Eric at her right, Ashley positioned Nichole behind them. They stepped backward to try to force the confused woman back into the building.

"Why are you here? What is that?" Nichole shouted over the demon's screams.

"Tarma," Ashley answered. As one landed and folded its enormous wings, another circled overhead and then swooped. Two. There was no way they could fight off two. "And Lena."

Demons. Their skin covered in scales, dark and slick, glistened like ebony in the distant streetlights. After Tarma landed, she clacked her jaws; it sounded like cracking bone.

When the second landed, both creatures shifted into human forms. "Sisters, we need to talk." Tarma reached out her hands.

"You've left us. Without word. We were worried," Lena said as they both stepped forward.

"Aw." Nichole started toward them. "We're fine, really."

"No." Ashley tried to push the infuriatingly innocent woman behind her again. "They want to kill you. Go inside."

The women kept coming. They were barely three yards away. "The Mother wishes only to know you are cared for," Tarma said.

Lena finished, "As she does with all of her children. You are her child, Nichole. You always will be. We care for you."

"We accepted you."

"We love you."

Two yards away. Both women reached out now. "There is no need to be frightened."

Nichole ducked under Ashley's arm and reached for the women. Ashley cried, "No!"

In a blink, demons stood in the women's places.

Eric roared. And in an instant, he shifted into what could only be called a giant wolf. He attacked Lena with claws and teeth. His gun was forgotten. Ashley wanted to stop him; his fur was so fragile compared to their scales.

Eric slammed his body into Tarma, sending her flying. Then he landed for an instant before leaping at Lena. Claws found their way under her scales and ripped as he wrenched, taking great gobs of flesh with them.

Lena landed a bite on his shoulder, but before she could bear down he raked his claws across an exposed eye and she roared in pain.

Half watching Eric's battle, Ashley wished she could help him. But she had to get Nichole to safety first. "Inside!" Ashley yelled, grabbing Nichole and pulling the innocent behind her once more.

When Ashley spun to face Tarma she found nothing.

"Ashley." The gurgled word came from behind her. Ashley spun, but it was too late.

Tarma had circled her and ripped out Nichole's throat.

Ashley screamed. Fury shook her body, and claws erupted from her own fingers. She leapt upon the back of the demon and tore at the leathery wings with every ounce of strength. The creature burst into the air and shook Ashley loose. She landed on top of Eric's gun. As fast as she could she aimed and fired, over and over, into the sky after the retreating demon.

She didn't realize the magazine had gone empty until Eric's calm hand covered hers and took the weapon from her. Deaf from the reports of the gun, she saw his lips move but couldn't hear what he said. She followed the motion of his hand and saw Lena, now in human form and torn to pieces.

She looked closer at him. He was covered in Lena's blood. He needed to get off the street. Behind her, Nichole gurgled again. Eric's predicament forgotten for a moment she knelt beside her former protégé, her friend, and wept. "I'm so sorry." She cradled the petite woman's body. "Oh, Nichole, I'm so sorry."

Nichole offered a faint smile before she slipped away.

• • •

Eric gave her a moment to grieve. But just that. The shots had alerted others who'd called the police. "Darling, we have to leave."

Sirens were getting closer. She wasn't budging. Eric did the only thing he could and called Aaron.

He gave him the address of the double homicide they'd attempted to interrupt and told him cars were already on the way. Luckily, Aaron hadn't yet gone home for the day and called dispatch, told them he was en route, and that there was an undercover already on the scene.

With the bottled water and napkins Ashley had in the car he cleaned his face the best he could and rinsed his mouth with water. A quick examination of Lena confirmed she wouldn't become some mutant werewolf-demon hybrid, if that was even possible. She had not survived his attack.

Ashley was still bent over her friend's fallen body when the police, and soon Aaron, arrived on the scene. Eric told and retold the lie he'd made up on the fly. She had been giving him a tour of the area when he saw the two women being attacked by a dark figure. They attempted to subdue the attacker, who got away. Ashley had tried to save her friend, and he tried to save the other one. "She seemed to be losing blood from every artery. It got all over me."

EMTs changed him into scrubs, and the police bagged his clothes. The wounds he'd sustained from the fight had already healed before he changed. His blood wouldn't register as human anyway, so they would toss it out as cross-contamination.

After Eric had changed, Aaron pulled him aside. "What's happening here, man? This is the place you investigated today, for the homicide. I read Max's report."

"Nothing to do with our investigation."

"I still think I should know." Aaron glanced around.

"Not here. We'll talk, off the record, in the morning."

"You've got four hours until morning, slick."

"Feds will be on the scene by then."

"Yes," Aaron said. His eyes narrowed at Eric.

"Did you get anything off the doll?"

"Two pieces of hair. Brunette. They are running them for DNA, but a match could take days. If he's in the system at all."

"Could be the victim's. Could be one of his other victims'. Could belong to the kid who stashed it under her pillow."

"Could be his. If we get a match, then you've cracked this case wide open."

"That would be nice." Eric ran a hand through his hair. Still caked with blood. "Then I can get home."

Aaron grunted. "Damn it, man, don't make me wait to talk around feds. What's happening here?"

"Fine. You want the truth?" Eric leaned in so his mouth was inches away from Aaron's ear. "She's a succubus, I'm a werewolf, and we just fought off two demons. One changed back into a woman, and the other got away."

Aaron's eyes were wild when he pulled away. "Fuck you, man. If you don't want to tell me, fine." He stalked away. The glance over his shoulder seemed more worried than angry.

It was practically dawn when they got back to the hotel room.

Ashley had been quiet the whole ride back. Her expressionless face stared straight ahead most of the time. Now and then she'd glance down to pluck at the dried blood on the hem of her shirt.

She'd jerked away every time the investigative unit tried to have her change, so they'd scraped and cut off what they needed while she cradled Nichole. Eric had had to hold her back while they bagged her friend's body. But even the struggle she put forth was half-hearted. When the life drained from Nichole's body, the fight drained from Ashley.

He turned the radio to an oldies station for the ride and didn't attempt small talk. Most likely, she didn't care what happened with the police, so he didn't fill her in.

She looked haggard and worn when they rode up in the elevator. About halfway up, she seemed to note her appearance. She straightened her clothes and combed her fingers through her hair. When the elevator doors opened, a peal of laughter from behind a closed door made her flinch.

No sooner did they enter his room than Ashley began to pace the floor.

"Are you okay?" he asked, though he knew full well that she wasn't.

"I killed her."

"No—" He stepped toward her.

"No." She held up her hand to stop him. "I left her. I knew she was in danger. So what did I do? I left her in the care of an innocent teacher, in a school full of innocent girls. Then what did I do? I led them straight to her. They couldn't find her. They needed me. They used me," she cried. "They *used* me."

She stormed to the window, opened the curtains, looked out over the Strip, and then closed them quickly. "Men will hurt you." She seemed to mimic someone. "They will lie to you, cheat you to get what they want, and use you." She coughed out a sob. "That's what the Mother would say." She began to shake with her tears.

"It's what they all said. But they were no better than what they said men were.

He wanted to help, but in the face of her pain, all he could do was try again to wrap his arms around her. This mother creature wouldn't let this be the end of it. Ashley was a loose end. At just the thought of the woman in his arms in danger, he could feel the beast within him fight to surface.

Once the weeping subsided, he said, "They will be coming for you next."

"Yes," she said, her face still pressed against his chest.

"The question is: how did they track you?"

Her brow furrowed. "I tracked you by following the bit of me that had become a part of you. But I could see it. Nichole could see the part of you in me. If the Mother or Tarma left a part of themselves *in* me or Nichole, I would be able to tell. So that can't be it." She shook her head and paced away. Shoving her hands in her pockets she stopped and her eyes widened. Slowly, she pulled her hand out. When her fingers opened he could see a black onyx ring in her palm, just like the one she wore.

She placed Nichole's ring on the dresser. "That's got to be how they are doing it," she said, unable to look away from it.

He took her shoulder and made her face him. Then he lifted her chin so he could look into her eyes. "Well then take it off."

Chapter 12

It was simple enough. Slip off the ring. She knew what Tarma and the Mother were now. The sisterhood wasn't the blessing she'd believed for so many decades.

She knew all of this, and yet she couldn't let it go. The power and the sense of purpose had sustained her all of this time. No matter its origin, it saved her when she needed it. Removing the ring felt like turning her back on it and throwing it away.

Eric watched her expectantly. To him, it was the logical choice. He would probably give up being a werewolf in a second.

Nichole had done it. She'd given it up without a moment's hesitation. For Nichole, the choice was simple—she'd wanted to be happy, she hadn't needed power, she'd known the right path when she saw it, so she leapt.

If I had chosen when Nichole had, she would still be alive.

Tears rose again, and Ashley blinked them away. She wouldn't hesitate anymore. She gripped the band and tugged. It wouldn't move. No matter how she twisted and wriggled, the black band seemed permanently attached.

"What's wrong?" Eric asked, shifting his weight from one foot to the other as if readying to launch himself into a brawl.

"I can't get it off." The indecision of a moment ago was replaced by panic. Suddenly, ridding herself of the cursed thing meant immediate life or death. She ran into the bathroom, selected the complimentary bottle of lotion, and squirted it on the ring. Pulled and twisted. She dug her nails under the band and tugged.

She shifted to an extremely overweight person, and the ring expanded. Then she shifted to a child. She yanked. With every shift, the ring shifted with her. Fat, thin, big, little. Maybe if she shifted and pulled fast enough, at just the right time …

Finally, Eric's arms reached into the flurry of images and caught her shoulders. "Easy," he whispered. "We'll figure something out."

"You were right. They'll come after me next. They're probably hunting me down now." She rested her head against his broad shoulder. Even in her current state she realized he was the steady force she wanted. If only she could give up the ring, the power, the strength.

But, if they caught up to her, they would find him as well. "I have to leave."

He caught her arm even as she turned away. "Not a chance." He scooped her off her feet.

"You're in danger."

"So what if I am? It wouldn't be the first time." After he placed her on the bed he opened the mini fridge and passed her a bottle of water. "Besides, I don't know if you were watching me tonight, but I think I handled myself rather well."

The cool water eased her aching throat. He *had* torn Lena to shreds. He handled himself so well that Tarma had fled rather than try to take them both on. He'd saved her life tonight. "You were amazing."

He smiled at the compliment even as he answered his ringing phone. He listened for a few minutes and then said, "I'm on my way." To her, he said, "Another girl was taken. I have to go." She began to stand, but he laid a hand on her shoulder. "No, you should stay here."

She took his hand in her own and stood. "They can get to me here."

"There is surveillance all over the place in this hotel." He waved his free hand toward the ceiling. "Nothing can happen without it being seen and recorded."

"They can change their appearance. They can be anyone. Surveillance won't make a difference. They could look like a senator if they wanted to." She laid a hand on his cheek. "They could look like you."

He closed his eyes for a moment. "Fine, but you'll need to be in disguise."

It took some negotiation. He insisted she use a form she'd never used before. Finally, he took out his phone and flipped to a picture of his old partner. "This is my old partner. Can you be her?"

She looked at the phone and smiled. He had to be joking. "We are going to a crime scene, and you want me to look pregnant?"

"Oh." The irritation packed into that word, coupled with the way his brow furrowed as he flipped for a different picture, struck her as funny. Despite the seriousness of their situation and the hell of the last twenty-four hours, she couldn't help but laugh quietly.

"Use this one of her," he said, handing her the phone again and rolling his eyes as she struggled to quell the fit of giggles.

When she got a hold of herself, she reviewed the picture and passed the phone back. "I'll wait to change until we're in the car." She waved her hand like he had. "There are eyes everywhere, and we don't want people thinking you've got a harem stashed in your room."

• • •

At the stoplight just before the upscale Henderson neighborhood he glanced at her. He did a double take. It was as if Lydia were sitting shotgun, just like old times. "Uncanny. Do you sound like her, too?"

"I could, but I've never met her," Ashley said. Then she frowned. "Will that be a problem?"

He thought for a minute. "No, it's fine. None of them have either." He made the turn. "Still, I'd rather introduce you as an assistant with another name."

"Rose Bailey," she said. And when he shot a look in her direction, she explained, "I had an elderly neighbor once. She would feed me when no one else could be bothered. It was her name."

"Okay, *Rose*, just follow my lead and let me do the talking, okay?"

"Not a problem. I don't have any delusions of being a detective."

Eric pulled the car in behind a black and white with its lights on. A quick survey of the street revealed the feds had already arrived.

Another child stolen from the home of a wealthy family. Was the kidnapper simply becoming more refined in his tastes? They exited the vehicle and Eric muttered, "Here we go."

They approached the uniformed officers stationed at the front door, and Eric displayed his ID. "We were called to consult by Detective Decker."

After a moment of close examination, the officer nodded to a man in a suit who stood just behind him. This man spoke into a walkie-talkie. A short while later, the door opened, and Aaron motioned for them to enter.

To his credit, Aaron didn't hesitate a beat when Eric introduced Ashley as his assistant, Rose, though his gaze swept over her before he led them upstairs. Did his eyes hesitate while looking at her abdomen? Did Aaron recognize Lydia and say nothing? Faced with that level of trust, Eric knew he should trust Aaron in return. However, the stretch would still be greater on Aaron's part. Believing in werewolves wouldn't be easy.

"Victoria Gunderson, twelve, disappeared from her bedroom between midnight and four a.m." Once again, Aaron knew the way through the maze of hallways, so he led the way. "She stayed up late watching a movie with her parents, and then when her mother was up in the middle of the night and saw her door closed she decided to check on her and found nothing. She is similar to the other girls who were taken in hair, eyes, and general facial and body structure.

"Crime scene unit has gone over the room already, but let's not disturb anything if we can avoid it." He handed them gloves and booties to go over their shoes. Once they were properly garbed he opened the bedroom door. "I think he was caught by surprise with this one."

Where Olivia's room had been decorated in pastels, Victoria's was done in earth tones. The effect was peaceful. A yoga mat lay in the middle of the floor on one side of her bed. In a far corner stood an overstuffed easy chair. An entire wall held a wide variety of books and what appeared to be fantasy statues, unicorns, and dragons. On the floor near the chair, standing on its pages as if dropped, was a book with a blue cover.

Ashley crossed the room to it. A yellow marker with a number two stood beside the book. Aaron cleared his throat as she bent to retrieve the book. Her fingers paused in midair. She gripped them into a fist and read the spine of the book aloud. "*Witch Way to Turn*, by Karen Y. Bynum." She looked at the men, then back at the book. "We need to leave it?"

"Yes," they said together.

Where Victoria's life was similar to Olivia Koburn's, it differed from Suzie Hogan by leaps and bounds. If it weren't for his nose, Eric wouldn't believe the three kidnappings and Susie's murder were connected. The only evidentiary way to connect them was the dolls. Not that anything about the dolls had proven traceable either.

"Did we find a doll?" Eric asked.

"Yes. Dressed for bed." Aaron turned to face the bed.

The bed hadn't been touched. It looked like the kidnapper had interrupted her reading. But the book was not the only thing out of place. Several of the girl's shoes were scattered away from the wall where three other pairs were aligned. "They struggled."

Aaron nodded.

"Where was the doll found?"

Aaron raised a finger. "That's why I think she did some damage when she fought back. The working theory is that he leaves the doll where he finds them. Susie, on the street. Olivia, sleeping in her bed. Victoria's doll was found propped at an awkward angle against the shelving here." He indicated a yellow marker with a black number one on it. "It was dressed in a blue nightshirt and gray sweatpants. Her mother confirmed it resembled what she wearing at the time of her disappearance."

"He expected her to be sleeping. That's why she surprised him." Ashley could visualize a dark figure sneaking into the room only to find his intended prey reading and not as easy to capture as he thought.

Eric nodded, his eyes somber, but his approval of her statement evident in the small twitch in the corner of his mouth. It warmed her.

"The drapes are blackout curtains," Aaron said. "He had no idea she was still awake until he'd already gotten inside. We found no blood or hair, so she didn't get him as good as we would hope. But she stood her ground and made enough ruckus that he dropped the doll here, rather than leave it in the chair or tuck it into bed. He grabbed her and left in a hurry. She struggled, but he fought to take her anyway. Either he really wanted her, or"—he raised an eyebrow—"she saw him and he couldn't risk her identifying him."

"If she knew her kidnapper that would give us a lead at least. Otherwise, we know how this will end," Eric practically growled. A cool hand rested on his arm. With a glance into Ashley's eyes he knew she shared his hurt.

Memories of his attack began to surface. The dim warehouse. Moving through the pallets of newspaper stacked ten feet high. His gun was at the ready, but his quarry moved more silently than a movie ninja. There was a tap on his shoulder. He spun.

"Eric?" It was Aaron. "Are you all right? Do you need some air?"

"No, I'm fine." He waved away the concern. To Ashley, he whispered, "Later."

Aaron glanced at the empty doorway and then stepped closer to Eric. "What's going on here? Rose? I've seen pictures of your old partner. Who is this girl? Do you want to clue me in?"

"This isn't the time." Another look at Aaron's face and Eric cleared his throat. "You wouldn't believe most of it. Let's just say she's got some talent when it comes to detective work. If anyone asks, she is a consultant from my end."

• • •

Aaron's suspicions put Ashley on edge. What could he be thinking? He was a decent enough man. He'd killed before, but she could also see he took no pleasure in it. His virtues overshadowed his sins. She wouldn't have looked at him twice when she was hunting for the sisterhood. Still, if he threatened Eric, she'd drain the cop without a second thought.

Aaron's stony gaze swept over both of them. "Fine, for now." He pointed at Eric. "We're going to have a long talk."

"Okay." She allowed Eric to make his promise. She didn't know Aaron, but she trusted Eric to make the best call for them.

"Soon."

"Count on it."

The three of them turned to face the scene. Eric muttered, "He didn't bother with a note this time."

Aaron crossed his arms. "No, if she caught him off guard maybe he didn't feel he had the time."

"Excuse me." A man in a dark blue uniform and bright blue booties covering his shoes tapped a knuckle on the door jam. "We need to sweep the room."

"Again?"

"Mr. Gunderson insisted."

Nodding, Aaron led them from the room.

Once they were in the hall, a crew of crime scene techs filed into the bedroom, each holding another piece of equipment. Ashley said, "Mr. Gunderson must have considerable influence."

Aaron grunted. "You could say that."

Eric led the way down the hall. "Let's see if we can ask the parents a couple of questions."

The first floor of the house was still swarming with federal agents. Taking pictures. Talking to servants. Talking to each other. Many of them stopped their conversations to watch the trio descend the stairs. When they reached the bottom, the conversations resumed, more quietly.

"They are interviewing the family in the father's home office."

Even as they approached the room Ashley's mouth began to water. Someone in that room was depraved. The stench of it billowed through the door. Her ring burned. Her eyes fogged.

Eric gripped her arm. "Are you all right?"

"Someone in that room is corrupt." Her voice was hoarse with the need to feed. "I don't know ... if I can control myself." She looked into his eyes and saw his confusion. "You know I feed on sin ... " She gasped. "It's unbearable."

He nodded and handed her the keys. "Wait in the car."

• • •

When he caught up with Aaron, Eric nodded in the direction Ashley went. "She felt sick."

Aaron nodded. "It's a difficult case."

They moved quietly to the corner of the room. They stood behind two overstuffed easy chairs separated by a small table and lamp. Eric's first thought as he saw the study was that his grandmother would love to have a room like this.

The walls were lined with bookcases and filled with books. Reference books behind the heavy wooden desk, classics and varieties of fiction along the other three walls. Judging by the colors of the spines and the size, many were romance paperbacks. Stained-glass transoms, dark because of the hour, topped several of the bookcases.

The girl's mother and another man who patted her hand sat on a small spindly couch in front of the bookcases.

Behind the desk sat, Eric presumed, the father of the girl. A fed and Aaron's boss occupied the visitors' chairs, while what appeared to be another fed stood off to the side. Every so often, he would narrow his eyes and write something. He emitted an air of suspicion. It was a tactic. Someone for the father to focus on aside from the questions. *The better to trip you up, my dear,* Eric thought.

The girl's father didn't squirm. He was poised, yes, but behind the air of control, something that must've been a habit for the powerful man, was the panic of a distressed father—a crease between his eyes that never smoothed, hands that maintained a death pinch on either end of a gold pen.

After ten minutes or so the pacing agent received a nod from the female doing the questioning and left the room. As he passed, the air currents wafted in Eric's direction. A familiar scent caught his attention. The killer had either been in the room recently, or he was still here.

How could Eric scan the room? The pacing tactic had been done and discarded. The father had officially moved to the category of victim's father. Eric glanced at Aaron and motioned for the two of them to leave the room.

Aaron's eyes widened as they rounded the corner. "Seriously, what's going on? He was making an enemies list. There are probably dozens of leads in those names."

"The feds will make you a copy."

Aaron continued to stare.

"Or at least they will be tracking down the leads themselves. Look, I need you to trust me one more time. I think our guy is in that room." At Aaron's sharp intake of breath Eric held up a hand. "I know I'm on thin ice with you as it is, and if I could explain everything now I would."

Aaron's face didn't twitch.

Eric chuckled softly. "I forgot what a good poker face you have." He considered a short version and dismissed it. This wasn't the place to debate the paranormal. "I'll tell you everything over coffee as soon as we're done here."

No reaction.

"Dude." Eric glanced over Aaron's shoulder to the three agents still outside the office. "We *really* can't talk about it here. It's the best I got."

Aaron ran a hand through his hair. "Fine. How do we find out if you're right?"

"I need a plausible reason to circle the room."

Aaron nodded. "How many times?"

"Just once. I need to get close to everyone for a second."

Eric's oldest friend stared at him, seeming to search his eyes for the reason behind his words. "Fine," he said again, "but when we're done I want a big-ass coffee and not some pussy espresso."

Eric clapped Aaron's shoulder. "Deal. Now how do I get around the room?"

"That's easy enough."

When they reentered the office, the man who had sat beside the wife had stepped to the right-hand corner of the desk. Mr. Gunderson had begun to ask questions of his own. Although he wouldn't appreciate it, an interruption would keep him from working himself up.

Aaron walked up beside the agent who sat in a visitors' chair. "Excuse me. I'm Lieutenant Aaron Decker and this is my associate, Detective Eric Adams."

Hellos were exchanged, and Eric moved to shake everyone's hand.

The FBI agent was clean. So were the father and mother. Though, from the wobble and the faint botanical smell on the mother's breath, she'd washed down an anxiety pill with gin.

The man who stood at the right-hand corner of Mr. Gunderson's desk stepped up and extended a hand.

HIM.

This man, with his expensive Italian suit, smooth face, and neatly trimmed dark, wavy hair, was the man who'd kidnapped the girls. This businessman had killed Suzie Hogan and who knew who else. "Hello, I'm Irving Pilcher, Mr. Gunderson's Chief Operations Officer."

Eric forced himself not to growl as he gripped Pilcher's cool, dry hand. "Sorry to meet you under these circumstances."

The man nodded. "Are you the team who've been trying to find the other missing girls on this case?"

"Yes."

Pilcher nodded again and stepped to stand beside Mr. Gunderson and put a hand on the father's shoulder. "Russell, these men have been trying to track this guy down and are stymied." To the FBI agent, he said, "I trust the FBI is in control of the investigation." Then he locked eyes with Eric.

Mr. Gunderson said, "Of course, we will appreciate any help you can offer."

Aaron passed a card to the FBI agent and laid one on the desk. "We will help in any way we can."

As they left the room Pilcher's voice could be heard, followed closely by the FBI agent assuring that while they wouldn't alienate any possible recourse they were in charge of the investigation now.

Aaron and Eric exited the front of the home. Aaron hissed, "Thanks a lot."

Eric glanced around and caught sight of Ashley standing next to the car. "Look. Do what you've got to do, then lead the way to breakfast. We'll give you that explanation."

"It's Saturday." Aaron glanced toward the sky brightening in the east. "Viv is always up with the sun. Come to my house for breakfast. She'll never let me hear the end of it if you don't stop by while you're in town."

Eric checked the sky as well. The setting moon was almost full. He had about four days to bring this guy in before Lydia went into labor. He could see Ashley patiently sitting in the car.

Aaron shifted his stance and caught Eric's attention. Eric said, "I think I can speak for both of us; after a night like tonight your wife's cooking sounds like heaven."

• • •

Aaron lived in a smallish house on a street filled with others just like it. The yard was trimmed, and a variety of flowering cacti filled the beds. With the low humidity and the nearly constant breeze it was easy to forget they were in a desert.

As they followed Aaron into the house, Ashley whispered, "Good people live here."

From the entryway, the scent of baking cinnamon and fresh coffee greeted them. "Vivian is the best cook," Eric said.

"Does your nana know that's what you think?" Vivian's lime-green apron would have seemed out of place on most people, however, on the radiant woman, it worked.

"Best after her, of course." Eric pretended to stammer as he returned her embrace.

She lifted her head from his shoulder. "Who's this?" she asked as she offered a hand to Ashley.

"Um," Ashley said.

"Yes." Aaron set a briefcase on the sofa just inside the living room and turned to Eric. "Would you like to introduce us to your companion?"

"My name is Ashley Paulo." She shared a glance with Eric, who nodded. "I'm a member of a sisterhood of succubae."

"And I've been a werewolf for the past year."

"Oh." Vivian smiled. "Well, I hope you're okay with apple cinnamon pancakes for breakfast, or maybe you'd like bacon and eggs, or better yet"—she patted Eric's chest—"I could defrost a chicken." Still giggling, she left the room.

Vivian had reacted as most people would. Aaron, on the other hand, stood as if flash-frozen, his eyes wide, his hands still holding the newspaper he'd brought into the house.

"You're not serious." He crossed the room and placed the paper on the coffee table. Still facing the paper, he spoke, "There's no such thing—well, Viv watches these shows—reads some books. It's not real." He turned to face them. "It's not real."

"Okay, it's not." Eric clapped his friend on the shoulder and squeezed. "You wanted to know, and I told you. I can't force you to believe me." He squeezed again before turning away. "Let's go get some of that breakfast." He tried to step past his friend to the door Vivian had used.

Aaron didn't move. "But—"

"I can convince him," Ashley said, stepping between them.

"Are you sure?" Eric asked.

"There's no way he'll really believe us otherwise. We know who the killer is. And there's no catching this guy alive without backup." She didn't need to go into the way they would have to stop him without Aaron's help. Ever the cop, Eric could bring people to justice, but extracting it on his own took a coldness he didn't have.

"What do you mean by that?" Aaron asked.

"You want him to face justice. If we go it alone, that won't happen." Her voice was hard as stone.

"You'll kill him," Aaron said.

"Worse. And even with you ready to scoop him up I can't say I won't do irreparable damage." She shook out her shoulders.

There was a long lull broken only by Viv's humming and the occasional clatter in the kitchen.

"I'm a sister succubus," Ashley continued. "I can change my form in order to attract prey."

Eric circled her to stand at Aaron's side. If he was startled, he might draw the weapon holstered at his side. Even Eric's quick reflexes might not be able to stop the reaction.

She made the change slowly. Eric recognized the woman as the one they'd raced through the night to save. Nichole.

"Wa—" Aaron started, his voice about two octaves too high.

"Steady," Eric muttered.

Even as a tear rolled down her cheek, she darkened her skin to that of a perfect chocolate chip cookie and shifted her features to simulate Vivian.

"Viv?" Aaron stammered.

"Yes, dear?" came the response from the kitchen.

"Uh … Is breakfast almost ready?"

"A few more minutes, but you can come pour some coffee if you want."

Even as the real Vivian responded to her husband, Ashley was already changing into a replica of Eric. The real Eric winked.

When she'd shifted back into her version of Lydia she stopped and leaned against the arm of the couch for a second. Both men stepped toward her. She released a weak laugh. "It's harder than it used to be."

Eric's smile faded, and he stepped even closer.

Ashley raised a hand. "I'm fine."

• • •

His eyes held only concern. He was too close. Hunger built within her—not for food, and not for his soul. She couldn't remember the last time she'd felt this kind of hunger.

Had his shoulders always been so broad? Had his eyes always seen into her heart? She reached a hand to touch Eric's face. A night's growth of beard prickled her fingertips. Had his lips always looked so inviting?

As he leaned closer, Eric whispered, "You're beautiful."

She'd been told that by countless men over the years. Mostly prey. And none of them had been talking about anything other than her looks. Eric's words meant something. A flush filled her cheeks.

His lips, soft and warm, pressed against hers. Her body reacted instantly. Libido, long dormant, inflamed every inch of her. She slid her hand to the back of his neck and pulled him closer. The kiss deepened. The room, the horrors of the past few days, everything slipped away as their bodies pressed against each other.

"Hey." The voice seemed so far away. "Hey." It sounded again like the insistent droning of a mosquito. "I hate to break this up, but Viv could walk in at any second, and you don't look a thing like you did a second ago."

Ashley glanced into the mirror, and a face she hadn't seen in a long time looked back at her.

"Hello?" Aaron stalked toward them. "Whenever you're ready?" His widened eyes emphasized his hoarse whisper.

Eric kissed the top of her head and released her. Once again, she shifted into Lydia. Just in time.

"Did you want coffee? I have tea." Vivian saw them in the foyer. "You're not leaving?"

"No, Ashley felt faint and was going to get some air," Eric replied.

"Oh, dear." Vivian started forward and took Ashley's hand. "You look so pale. When was the last time you ate?" Without waiting for a response she steered her into the other room. "Dig in."

They all sat, and Vivian set a pitcher of orange juice on the table before sitting across from Ashley. The conversation turned to catching up for the old friends.

"How is your grandmother?" Vivian asked Eric, as she spooned some fruit onto Ashley's plate.

"Nana's great," Eric said, forking a couple pancakes onto his plate beside several strips of bacon. "She spends her days divided between her garden and her kitchen. When I told her I was coming out here she told me to say hi and invite you to come visit."

"That sounds like a great idea. Aaron's due for a vacation soon. Perhaps we'll convince him to take it. We definitely won't get a chance to travel once Ricky starts school."

"How old is he now?"

"Three. And he already wants to be a detective like his daddy." Viv smiled warmly at her husband.

Rapid footsteps sounded on the ceiling. "Speak of the devil and he shall awaken." Viv made two plates and stood, lifting them both. "I'll take him into the den for breakfast so you three can talk."

"That's okay," Aaron began, but she shut him up with a peck on the lips.

"I know when you need to talk shop." She carried the plates from the room. The little pounding feet made their way down the stairs. They could hear a piping voice call for mommy before giggles and more running. A door closed on the other side of the house.

Aaron sighed and said to no one in particular, "I'm a lucky man."

After a moment, Eric broke the silence. "Irving Pilcher is our guy. We need to find a way to lure him in."

"Why would the COO of Gunderson's empire want to kidnap, torture, and kill young women?"

Ashley grunted softly. "Just because he's rich doesn't mean he isn't capable of extreme evil."

Eric nodded. "Some would say he would be more capable."

Aaron shook his head and ate a bit of cantaloupe before responding. "His life is so public. How could he possibly do this for so long without anyone knowing about it?"

Ashley gripped her orange juice. "His sort of fantasies don't grow in the light of day. They build in the corners of his mind until they darken his soul. The darker it gets, the more likely he is to act on what he truly wants."

"How do you know it's Pilcher?"

That was the question, wasn't it? He'd seen what Ashley could do; would he believe his old friend could be a supernatural beast?

"I smelled him," Eric said. He took a bite of bacon and smiled, showing nothing of the unease Ashley knew boiled under the surface.

"Because you're a werewolf?" Aaron's gaze shifted between the two of them. "Even with her show, it's hard to believe."

"Why do you think I'm not a cop anymore? I can smell better than any police dog. It's as good as seeing. I couldn't explain how I knew where a pedophile was hiding his latest victim. I knew who'd committed murder, rape … and who was lying. Did you know you smell different when you lie? But as a cop, I had to give cause. I had to find 'real' evidence. Quite often, there wasn't any, or when there was, it was so minute, no one should have found it. No one questions a PI as long as they deliver. I haven't had a case yet that I couldn't solve. You know that. It's why you brought me here."

Aaron sipped his coffee, then rubbed a hand over his face. "You've been this way for a year?"

Eric nodded.

"It's going to take a while to process. I'm sorry." He stood then and walked to the kitchen window. In the silence, they could hear a television in the other room. A child's song was playing, and a tiny voice piped gibberish to the melody. Finally, the song ended with "Yeahs" and clapping from Ricky and Vivian. Aaron nodded as if in agreement.

"I don't need to know any more. I'm not sure I want to. Whatever you claim to be, you both are on my side and that's all that matters." To Eric, he said, "You're a brother. I believe you, no matter how outlandish it sounds."

They stood, clasped hands, bumped shoulders, and slapped each other's backs in a kind of man-hug.

Once everyone got settled Ashley cleared her throat. "So, how do we catch this guy?"

Aaron cleared his throat. "I can't put a tail on him or get a warrant for his house without approval … " He glanced across the table at Eric.

"But we can." Eric nodded. "We'll stop by his house this afternoon and tail him when goes to visit his victims. Then we can call in a tip."

"Can you tail him without being seen?"

Eric leveled a gaze at his old friend.

"Okay." Aaron smiled. "Do your reconnaissance. Make sure there's proof we can use. Then call in the tip, and I'll bring the cavalry."

•••

They had several hours before they planned on trailing Pilcher. Given their evening, Eric suggested they return to the room to sleep. He knew they both could use it.

Once inside, they didn't say a word. He sat on the edge of the bed to remove his shoes. When he stood and faced Ashley she'd already slipped out of her jeans and had shifted so she was wearing a baggy t-shirt that just barely covered white cotton panties. She was still in the image of his partner.

"What do you look like?" he asked, seeming to startle her from her own thoughts.

"I look like anything I want." She didn't seem to understand, but he suspected she did.

"You. The real you." He pulled off his belt, rolled it up, and placed it on the dresser.

"You've already seen the real me." She climbed into the bed.

If she could get comfortable for bed, so could he. There was something strangely dirty about climbing into bed with Lydia, though. "Have I?" He pulled off his shirt, but she was still on the bed, as his old partner, and he stopped.

She saw him hesitate.

Then he sighed. "It seems wrong when you look just like my partner."

At this, she smiled. Her first real smile since the day before. Slowly, she shimmered into what he took to be herself. Brown hair with gold highlights and a couple of silvery hairs that glinted slightly in the light of the bedside table. A round face with a dimple in the left cheek. Eyes that were so light brown they were almost golden. Her body had curves. The good kind. In all the right places.

"Wow." Suddenly he was more than a little self-conscious about removing his jeans.

"What?" She shimmered again, her appearance starting to blur.

"No." He climbed onto the bed and took her hand. "I like it." He looked her over again. "You are so hot."

She solidified into herself. "Really?"

"Oh, yeah," he breathed as he leaned in to kiss her. He'd never seen a sexier woman. She was it. She was the one. Would she understand what it meant? He breathed deep. She needed to understand. She had to agree to forever. Silently, he prayed she would.

Nervous, more than he'd ever been, he leaned back, keeping a hold on her hand. "Will you marry me?"

•••

He wasn't kidding. He wanted her, and he meant forever. There would be no backing out of it for him. She wanted to laugh. He couldn't see it, but they had shared so many pieces of themselves with each other already that they wouldn't be easily separated anyway. The pieces of him completed her more than when she was whole.

Her answer had already been written the instant she ran from the sisterhood with Nichole. This man was her future, and she was his. Finally, he knew it, too.

She took his face in her hands. "With all of my soul, forever."

He laughed and kissed her. Passion that had been held in control seemed unlocked, and the world fell way. Nothing mattered but them. Kissing, stroking, they shared everything. He opened his soul so completely to her, and she responded in kind.

They sank into what seemed like dozens of feather pillows on the bed. His voice was husky. "You have such an amazing body."

She warmed at the comment. And choked on a small sob.

"What is it?" he asked.

"You see *me*."

"No matter who you pretend to be, I will always see *you*." He gathered her in his arms and traced his fingertips lightly down her back.

His male scent mingled with the light fragrance of soap from an earlier shower.

Continuing to hold her in one arm, he caressed her with his other hand, starting at her neck. As he brushed her hair back from her shoulder he leaned down and touched his lips to hers.

Gentle but not hesitant, his hands explored her. Behind every movement, she felt purpose. Slow. Sensual. Needing to focus on something other than the areas of her skin screaming to be touched, she closed her eyes and reached for him. Her fingers traced his hard chest, running across his abdomen, which rippled as he shifted to stroke her thigh.

He leaned over her, kissing her hair, cheeks, nose, lips. His magic hands braced him as he hovered over her, raining kisses down over her neck and shoulders.

She knew he was taking it slow, taking care that their first time would be special. She wasn't a virgin, but her last encounter had been decades before and hadn't been tender. She became aware of her entire body as he kissed and caressed it. Not just the key areas.

Her hands moved as well, caressing the muscles of his arms and back. They rippled as he moved.

Oh, the anticipation. Each breast received a kiss, then he traced them with his tongue in a closing spiral, and finally flicked his tongue across the tip. She gasped and arched toward him. Didn't he know this was driving her crazy?

He moved on, lightly brushing his lips against her stomach. She moaned in protest, reaching for him, running her fingers through his hair.

"Are you in a hurry?" She could barely make out his mischievous grin though the veil of lust clouding her vision.

"I need you," she whispered, wanting his touch more than anything she'd ever wanted.

He touched his lips to hers again. She felt his smile and wrapped her arms around his neck before he could move on and continue the sensuous torture.

Sinking into the kiss, she felt the weight of his body on hers. The earth spun, and her senses swam, then he ran a hand down her side and slipped a finger inside her. She cried out against his lips.

Once again, every touch became slow and deliberate. His fingers explored the inside and his thumb brushed the outside, working her to climax. Lights burst and flowed with colors of a turbulent aura. She cried out again and focused him in her vision. The world still whirled about him, but he was steady in her sight.

"I need you," she whispered again. The lust had gone, leaving only him and a void he would fill. And as he did, they seemed to fall through space, love, and time, heralded back to earth by a multitude of bells ringing.

• • •

He needed to take his time. To make it special for both of them. He'd always been able to drive a woman wild, and he had been worried for a minute he had lost his touch. Her reaction proved otherwise.

Her moans almost ended him right then. She reached for him, had tried give him some of the pleasure he was giving her, but he stayed just out of reach until the world swam. Then he entered her. She gripped every inch of him, wet and warm and pulsing. They moved together. Bodies moving to the rhythm of their heartbeats. Faster and faster, until ... light seemed to engulf them both and they gave their all to each other.

Their hearts slowed, and their breathing slowed. As they snuggled, they both knew they would never be alone again. They had become one.

Chapter 13

A quick internet search led them to Pilcher's house. As they drove through the neighborhood Ashley gripped her right hand over the onyx band on her left ring finger. At Eric's quizzical glance she pointed and said, "The sisterhood lives down that street."

"Maybe you should … " he began.

"I can't," she whispered, twisting the band and giving it an experimental tug. "Anyway, we need it." He knew that was an excuse. His sense of smell would get them far enough. The idea that she couldn't remove the ring nearly sent her into a panic, yet she seemed fearful of the opposite too.

He grunted. He didn't understand. Was it just because she didn't want to lose her powers? He would give up his abilities in a second, but he also knew she felt like they were the only things that empowered her.

They drove slowly past Pilcher's house. No one appeared to be home. Eric pulled into a driveway down the block on the opposite side of the street.

"Won't someone say something about us parking here?" Ashley asked.

"There's a for sale sign in the front yard and a lock box on the front door." He gestured toward the ornate door they faced. "No one parks on the street in this neighborhood if they can help it."

She nodded. "So, what do we do now?"

"There is no sign he's home. So we watch the house."

"Maybe we should check to see if he's keeping the kids there. If he is, we could get them out before he even gets home."

"He could be home and just parked in the garage."

"The point is, from here, we can't tell if he's home. The only way to know is to knock. That's why we got the props, isn't it? As she pulled a bag from the back seat she morphed into a young girl. She could have been a sister to any of the abducted girls. Her clothes changed with her. Now she was in a scouting uniform. She pulled a clipboard from the bag. She winked at him and moved to open her door.

He grasped her arm to stop her. "Will you be able to control yourself if he answers the door?"

She looked him in the eye, and for a second he could see doubt. Then her eyebrow arched. "You'll be there, Daddy. I promise to behave."

He rolled his eyes. "Don't call me Daddy."

"Dad?"

He grunted.

"Pop?"

"Cut it out."

They climbed out of the car and slowly walked up the street. When they got to Pilcher's house Ashley went up to the front door. Playing the father, Eric needed to hang back a bit. He measured the distance to the door. He could reach her in five bounds.

The front door opened to reveal a woman in her mid-to-late fifties. "Can I help you?"

"Good afternoon. My name is Michelle. I'm with the Desert Scouts. I'm selling cookies for my troop. Number 492." She saluted and then lifted her clipboard to show the woman a fake order form they'd downloaded that morning with several sales already listed. "As you can see there are several new cookies this year."

"Oh, how lovely. Come in."

Ashley feigned worry. "I'm not supposed to." She glanced back at Eric.

"Your father can come, too." The woman pitched her voice to carry so Eric could hear. "Come on in for a minute while I get my purse."

Eric reached Ashley, and they followed the woman.

Ashley whispered, "All I get from her is innocence with an undertone of mischief."

Eric leaned close to Ashley's ear. "She's not nervous, and he's not home."

"Have a seat, I'll be right back." The woman waved at the living room before continuing on her way. "Can I offer you some lemonade?" she offered.

Eric coughed. The last time a woman had offered him lemonade the perp he was tracking had killed her before she could hand him the glass. "No, thank you."

The sitting room at the front of the house was connected to a dining area by an opening in a half wall. On the other side of the dining room another half wall revealed the woman puttering around in the kitchen.

Over the mantle of the fireplace hung a group picture of Pilcher, his wife—the woman singing to herself in the kitchen—and a teenage girl, similar in appearance to the other victims. Nearly identical to Victoria Gunderson. On the back of the antique couch sat a row of rag dolls. Each dressed in a different outfit.

"I never have guests." Mrs. Pilcher reentered the room carrying a tray of butter cookies shaped like little flowers with a hole in the middle, which she placed on the coffee table. "These are so much fun." She placed a cookie on her finger and nibbled the edge.

Ashley passed her the order form. "I like your dolls."

"Oh, me too," Mrs. Pilcher agreed. "My husband used to make them for my daughter. They were so close, the two of them. Sometimes she'd have problems with her stomach, and he'd sit up with her all night." Tears welled, and the woman sniffled. "She died years ago, but he still makes them sometimes. He gives them away to little girls that remind him of her. A special little doll for a special little girl, he'd say."

Using her disguise to its advantage Ashley widened her eyes and asked, "Oh, how did she die?"

Eric scolded, "Sweetie, that's not polite to ask."

Mrs. Pilcher smiled gently. "Children are curious." She patted Ashley's head. "That's a good quality in children. We were in a car accident. I was in a coma for a month. When I woke up Irving told me that she'd passed. My poor darling. They were so close; he was devastated."

Absently, she finished the cookie she'd worn on her finger, then she slipped on another, and nibbled off that one as well. "I just love cookies, don't you?" she asked as she checked several boxes on the order form.

• • •

Once on the street, on the way back to their car, Eric said, "She had brain trauma. She's functional. So much so that she's probably fooling herself. I really don't think she even notices what Pilcher's doing."

Ashley nodded. "What I could see in her aura was almost childlike. She has an overwhelming innocence about her. I don't think she would be able to notice complex threats."

"How do you mean?"

"She wouldn't fear a growling dog."

"I'll try not to be offended."

"She's innocent. In every possible way. Her husband, though …"

"Isn't," he finished for her. "Yeah, I smelled him. I couldn't catch the scent of any of the girls, though. Looks like we'll have to follow him."

"Should we report the doll collection to Aaron?"

"He'd only be able to put a tail on him, if that. He might not be able to get approval for a tail based solely on a tip. He'd have to knock on her door, too. Ask some questions. Too much activity could spook Pilcher if he isn't spooked already."

They got into the car and waited. Before long, a sedan pulled into the driveway of the Pilchers' house.

"That's him." Eric twisted the rearview so he could watch the house but still face forward.

Pilcher glanced up and down the street before entering his house. After a moment, the porch light went out. Luckily, she was far enough away from the house that she didn't want to devour Pilcher's soul.

"Are we going to sit here all night?" Ashley asked, before shifting back to herself. Given the way they'd spent their day, she had a difficult time keeping her hands to herself.

"It's a stakeout." Eric patted her hand, which seemed to snake its way up his thigh. "The whole point is to pay attention to the subject."

"Right." She pulled her hand away. "Pay attention. But it doesn't have to be rapt attention. Does it?" She leaned over and kissed his throat, peppering it until she reached his far earlobe, and in doing so, she'd climbed into his lap.

"That feels wonderful, but—"

"And if we're like this I can keep an eye on them, can't I?" It was serious, she knew that. But the scent of Eric, and the memory of that morning, had her longing for a repeat performance. She'd never felt so close to anyone in her long lifetime. So connected and still so free.

For once, she felt nothing but love coming from a man. No lies. No agenda. It was invigorating. She wanted to make him feel as euphoric as he made her.

Eric smiled as he slowly stroked her arms. "Yes, but as soon as he begins to move we'll have to stop, and I *know* I won't want to do that."

"True." She shifted her hips in a slow circle and ran her fingers into his hair. "The upstairs window just lit up. It seems as though they are settling in for the evening."

Eric glanced into the rearview mirror. "So you're saying we have time to do a little of this?" He gripped her bottom and pulled her tighter to him. His hands slid under her shirt. They caressed her back and sides, then eased around front to cup her breasts. His warm thumbs circled over her nipples, hardening them.

"Oh." She leaned into his touch and bent to kiss him again. It would have been so easy to allow herself to forget the outside world as pleasure and fog clouded her mind. She opened her eyes for a moment to check Pilcher's house, only to see the lights on his car glow. "Shit. He's moving." She climbed off Eric's lap and watched as the dark sedan pulled away down the street. "Shit," she repeated.

"Keep an eye on him." Eric started the car and backed onto the street.

"He just turned right."

"Okay." They turned as well and pulled up behind Pilcher at a light to exit the neighborhood. Eric glanced at Ashley as she smoothed her hair and tried to get comfortable in her seat. "Told you so."

She grunted. "We didn't miss him." She gave his leg a squeeze. "I regret nothing."

"Neither do I." The depth of his voice told her he meant more than just playing around in the car while on a stakeout.

They followed Pilcher's sedan onto the highway. After a while, Eric said, "He'd want to keep his victim as far away from his home as possible."

"Makes sense." She nodded. "The wife is fragile. It seems he still values her, regardless of his extracurricular activities."

Their course took them away from the city. Twilight had them turning on the headlights. Luckily, they weren't the only ones on the road. For now.

She read a traffic sign. "He's heading toward Pahrump."

"That doesn't make sense. The problems there would be the same ones he'd have in Vegas. He couldn't hide the girls in a city, or even a suburban neighborhood. Not if he wanted to keep them alive."

As he spoke, the car they followed slowed and switched on his blinker. They followed suit. The exit had a gas station and a couple of fast food restaurants. He drove past everything. Then, after about five minutes, he pulled into a motel parking lot.

Eric didn't slow. As they passed, they could see Pilcher drive behind the building. Eric pulled into the first driveway after the motel and turned around.

Ashley reached out with her senses. She could feel the evil that was Pilcher. But also there were three other people. All innocent. All terrified. Something rose in her. Her ring grew hot. She could feel the power flow from that point and radiate throughout her body. "We've found them."

"We have to be sure," he said.

She remembered the pull she'd felt in the Gundersons' house and shivered. Eric was afraid of his own powers, of being a monster. What would his reaction to hers be? They had just found happiness. How would he react if she attacked Pilcher? "I don't think … I shouldn't."

"Just wait in the car. I'll scent out the girls." Eric cut the lights as soon as he pulled into the far side of the lot.

The closer they got, the stronger the pull. She closed her eyes but reopened them when he touched her arm. "Seriously, just wait here. I have to be sure the girls are here before we call in Aaron and the cavalry."

"Right."

He leaned over and brushed his lips against hers. "I'll be right back."

She watched him until he disappeared behind the back of the motel. The building had once been maroon, but years of bleaching in the sun-drenched desert left it a pale and somewhat sickly salmon.

The tugging had become painful. If she gave in, there was no telling what she'd do. In all her time in Vegas, she'd never thirsted so deeply for a man's soul. Before she realized it, she was out of the car and crossing the parking lot.

• • •

Eric didn't draw his gun, though his hand itched to have it ready. He couldn't confront Pilcher. *I only need to be sure I have the right place.* The sedan had been parked halfway down the length of the building. That was most likely where Pilcher was keeping the girls.

As he passed the doors to what seemed to be empty rooms, he sniffed and listened. No telling how many girls the man had taken. The first three rooms were empty, but Pilcher's scent was all over them. It was possible he'd once stored his captives there.

As he neared the middle, he did draw his weapon. The fourth room was occupied. Only one girl from what he could tell. He wanted to save her. To take her to safety before calling Aaron. But that could tip off Pilcher and put the other girls at risk.

A yelp split the air ahead. He moved quick and silent to the large window. A sliver of light peeked through the drapes. Behind the door a female screamed and begged. Even through the door Eric heard the punch that quieted her. He couldn't leave her. He couldn't call backup. He had to help these girls now.

He leaned back and kicked the door open. The wood of the door frame splintered. The door itself slammed against the wall. Pilcher sat on the edge of the bed still fully dressed. A shape shivered under the flower comforter beside him.

"Can I help you?" He was calm, as if the man who'd just kicked in his motel room door didn't faze him, and neither did his gun.

"Stand up and put your hands behind your back." Even after so long, his cop training took over. Eric couldn't kill the man in cold blood. He might not come quietly, but his evil would end.

Pilcher laughed. "I'll do no such thing." He stood and held his arms wide. "I'm unarmed. I own this property."

"You don't own these girls."

"No one wanted them. Living on the street. Even in their mansions, they weren't wanted. No one paid attention to them. Loved them like they needed to be loved. Until me.

"You know, I had a girl once. My wife and I. She was smart, but the smart ones always think they know what's best. She needed me to look out for her. Teach her.

"When my daughter died, I knew I had to replace her. All of these men with daughters they barely acknowledge. Those girls were to be looked at, like dolls. Then, I realized, they can have the doll. I want the girl."

While he was talking, the comforter moved down a bit. Eric could see the rope that tied the girl to the headboard. If he transformed, he'd frighten the girl worse. So Eric moved closer, stepping close to a small table near the door. He tried to angle his gun away from the girl.

"Put the gun away," Pilcher continued in his smooth tone. "You're not a monster. Leave me with my family."

"Turn around and place your hands behind your back."

"No."

• • •

Ashley turned the corner in time to see Eric enter the room. She approached the open door with as much speed and with as much restraint as she could muster. She couldn't let him go in alone, but

153

she didn't want to startle the poor child who cowered under the covers.

When Pilcher refused to follow Eric's direction, Ashley's thin thread of control snapped. Rage she'd never known before took over. She hurled herself through the motel room door. She pushed Eric aside. She saw only Pilcher and his fetid soul.

Chapter 14

Eric fell against the small table next to the door. His gun clattered to the stained linoleum floor and slid under the tattered fabric that skirted the box spring. He measured the distance in a glance, but before he could move to retrieve it, Ashley, the woman he loved, caught his attention with a scream.

She was shifting but not shifting. As she changed, so did her scent. From where he sat, transfixed, her skin rippled and then seemed to tear in millions of different places. Scales slipped through and into place covering her body from head to toe. Her body also changed. Her hands sported four-inch claws, and a delicate tail whipped from behind her. But the worst, and most terrifying, was her face. No trace of humanity remained. Her snout sported rows of fangs, just as black as her claws. Her eyes were like pools of tar, deep and endless.

•••

Ashley lifted Pilcher by the face, brought him close, and savored his delightful terror. Slowly, with sadistic delight, she exposed his soul a piece at a time, reaching in with her mind's claw over and over. Carving it away like peeling an onion. Layer by layer. Even wholesome events, work deals, benign shopping trips all tasted delicious. No matter what the Mother had told the sisterhood, Ashley knew them for lies. It wasn't about saving humanity from evil. It was about the harvest. Reaping the souls of those who the world wouldn't mourn. If wife-beaters, rapists, and killers disappeared without a trace, who would care? No one would look too hard. None but their mothers would mourn them, and most not even then.

Irving Pilcher had nothing below the evil. No part of him treasured his wife. No part believed the girls he held captive were anything more than the dolls he left in their place. So, she drained him. Every drop was gone, but her hunger hadn't abated.

Standing on the other side of the bed were a man and a girl. The girl was wrapped in the blanket from the bed. Their souls were intact.

They weren't nearly as sweet as the one she'd just finished, but she was hungry. She stepped closer and reached for the girl. The man trained his gun on her, and Ashley could only laugh.

"Don't make me do this," he said, his gun trained on her chest.

"That won't hurt me." She felt her teeth gnash together as she spoke, and she didn't entirely like it.

He shoved the girl out the door and closed it behind her. "Ashley, stop." He holstered his gun.

Something within her fought. Struggled against the wash of new impulses.

"I love you. We've mated, and for me, that's for life. If my life is to end now, at your hand, then so be it." He stepped closer. His fingers brushed against the scales of her face, causing her entire body to quake. "Let's live a bit longer, shall we?"

Ashley shuddered, and the creature that had taken such control over her subsided. She was still trembling when Eric wrapped his arms around her. Over the sound of her heart slamming in her chest, she barely heard him whisper into her hair that everything would be all right. How could it ever be all right? She'd lost control.

She panted like she'd run a marathon. The beast within her only wanted to feed. She had no power over it. She struggled to turn the short breaths into deep, cleansing breaths, to calm herself before she was completely overcome with nausea. Eric could easily have died at her hand and she could have done nothing to stop it.

"I don't know." She rubbed her hands against her face. "I don't know if I can control this."

Eric chuckled. "I know what you mean. We'll figure it out. Together." He opened the door and found Victoria Gunderson standing before them wrapped in a bed sheet, bloody from where her injuries had opened. When she saw the body of her tormentor on the ground she sobbed and ran to Ashley.

"Time to make the call," Eric said, glancing around to see if they'd left any obvious evidence.

Ashley nodded. "We have to leave. You can't tell anyone we were here."

The girl nodded.

"He's not dead, but he won't wake up." When the girl's eyes widened, Ashley took a lighter from the bedside table and held it under his wrist. The flesh turned black, and the man didn't even flinch. "We have to leave you with him," Ashley said by way of an apology.

The girl kicked the body. "When they ask me what happened, I'll tell them he was attacked by a dragon."

"That's just fine." Eric smiled and pulled out his cell phone. "The cops will be here soon to take you back to your parents." He led Ashley back to the car.

• • •

Aaron shook both of their hands warmly. "Don't be a stranger."

"I won't, I promise." Eric proceeded with a warm shoulder-bump hug.

"You know, you don't have to head home so soon. Even though he's a vegetable, it's an open-and-shut case. I'm worried about Victoria Gunderson, though—her statement involves a vivid description of a dragon." Aaron glanced Ashley's way. "You can't do dragons—never mind." He raised his hand when she cocked her head slightly, staving off her response. "I really don't want to know."

"We have to get back." Eric left out that the reason they had to leave was to deliver his ex-partner's werewolf baby. It wouldn't matter if Aaron's reaction was horror, disbelief, or curiosity. Now wasn't the time.

Aaron nodded and then shook Ashley's hand. "Pleasure to meet you."

Soon, Eric and Ashley boarded a flight to their new home.

• • •

Lydia was ready to pop. Ashley understood why Eric's ex-partner wanted him by her side. Although Lydia and Ryan had been strangely welcoming, Ashley felt like an intruder. Dishes were the least she could do.

"Sorry we don't have a dishwasher. I think we're one of the last families in America that doesn't.

"Oh, I don't mind. Really. You've been so welcoming," Ashley said as she donned rubber gloves.

"You're family now." Lydia smiled. "Before I met Ryan, I was alone. I had no plan for the future other than to look out for my career. Two years ago, if you had told me I'd be off the force, married to a man who I'm madly in love with, and about to have his baby, I'd have said you were crazy." She brought over the glasses from the dinner table. "But here I am. When you are—what we are—family takes on a different meaning. Never mind the supernatural part of it, though that *is* huge. It's a community, albeit a small one, to share your lives with. Now you're a part of it … whether you like it or not."

The memory of the Indian restaurant surfaced. "You'll have to ask him, but I think Eric found some more family in Vegas."

"Really?" Lydia's expression was wary, but from the way her eyebrows arched and the corners of her lips quirked, Ashley knew as soon as Lydia went in the other room that would be her first question.

Ashley smiled. She'd wanted a family all of her life; even decades ago, her biological family had been beyond dysfunctional. The sisterhood, which had filled the void for so long, had turned on her. These people seemed so accepting, if only she could fit here. But there was still something off. Not with them. With her. She was more of a danger than they could ever be.

"Eric misses being a cop," Ashley said, changing the subject as she rinsed the last plate and placed it on the drying rack. She took the glasses and submerged them in the soapy water. "Do you?"

"Not as much as I thought I would. Ryan still writes articles, so he works from home, and I've been getting ready for the baby." She rubbed her belly. "Perhaps one day I'll see if Eric wants a partner at his agency. For now, I can't really think beyond the baby. It's always on my mind."

"I can imagine. Eric said you will most likely give birth during this full moon."

Lydia took a deep breath and nodded. "It makes sense. So, sometime in the next three days."

"Thank you for letting me be a part of it," Ashley said quietly, her gaze focused on her task as she rinsed the last glass and drained the sink.

"Family," Lydia said again as she clapped Ashley on the shoulder. "Do you have one?"

"Not exactly." Did she dare explain? She'd barely opened her mouth to change the subject when something slammed against the kitchen window. A face materialized. Dark and fanged. Dark eyes seemed to focus on Ashley as the creature reared back and head-butted the window.

Tarma.

"What the hell is that?" A growl built in Lydia's throat only to end in a squeak. She huffed for a moment, gripped her stomach, and called for her husband. "Ryan!"

Glass cracked and wood splintered as the creature slammed against the window again. Ashley had only a second to grab Lydia's shoulders and steer the cursing woman away.

Glass shattered, spraying the room with shards. The demon screamed. Lydia roared. Both men ran into the kitchen. They had guns, equipped with silencers, leveled at Tarma and opened fire. The demon swiped at them and screamed louder than the gunfire. Ashley's ears rang in pain.

Ryan emptied his clip and reloaded. The black figure fell backward out of sight.

Everyone spoke at once, but Ashley couldn't hear any of them. Then Ryan held his hands out for them all to be quiet. After a few moments the ringing stopped.

"What the hell is she doing here?" Eric growled.

"You know her?" Ryan asked.

Eric nodded and looked at Ashley. "That was Tarma, wasn't it?" When Ashley nodded, Eric cursed again. He climbed onto the sink to look out the window. When he faced them, he said, "Aside from the blood on your siding, there's no sign of her."

"Who is she? Why did she attack?" Ryan asked.

"They're after me." Tears filled Ashley's eyes.

Ryan moved to be nose to nose with Eric. "They followed you here from Vegas?" His voice rumbled with his temper.

Eric nodded.

Ryan paused a moment before asking Ashley, "How did they track you?"

Lydia hummed.

Eric answered. "It's got to be the ring. She's tried to take it off, and she can't."

Ashley grasped the ring. Her indecision had endangered everyone. Lydia leaned against the refrigerator with her head down. The two men of action stared at her, standing in the middle of glass and blood.

Ashley stepped to Eric, glass crunching beneath her feet. "You are a hero," she told him. "With everything you are, in any form. It's time for me to be as brave as you." She glanced back at Lydia and then bowed her head. "I can't endanger my family." With that, she strode from the kitchen and into the night.

• • •

Eric and Ryan both moved to follow her, but Lydia's groan halted them both. "Were you hurt?" Ryan moved to his wife's side.

She panted and met his gaze through a curtain of hair. "I'm in labor. My water broke."

Eric stepped to her other side to support her. "Are you sure?"

"Unless the baby is popping champagne corks in there, yes, I'm sure."

A scream sounded overhead. Ryan kissed Lydia and then stepped back and checked the clip of his gun. To Eric, he said, "You're up."

"But—" Though one arm was tucked under Lydia's, his other hand held his gun.

She groaned, and her grip on Eric's shoulder tightened. Ryan moved back to her and held her up on her other side. When the contraction passed she shrugged out of their grips and barked orders like a general. "Eric, you have experience delivering babies. You're with me. Ryan, go. Protect our sister-in-law." She waddled into the other room, her wet pants clinging to her thighs with each step.

"Careful, Ashley can turn into one of those things, too," Eric warned. "She doesn't have control."

Ryan hesitated a second to glance after his wife, who had already stripped from the waist down. Her body shook as she breathed through another contraction, supported, in part, by her claws embedded in the doorjamb of the living room. "You've fought them before, what works best against them?"

"Teeth and claws," Eric answered. "But take this anyway." He passed Ryan the loaded weapon.

Ryan slipped the Glock into his belt and disappeared into the night.

"Eric?" Lydia barked.

He rolled up his sleeves and moved to assist his laboring partner.

• • •

The blood trail circled the house. Though Ryan and Lydia lived on the outskirts of town they had three neighbors within a half mile of the house. Trees would block the view, but the scream of the circling demon echoed off the surrounding hills. No one could miss that.

Ashley moved into a clearing behind the house. Moonlight seemed to bleach the beds of flowers and short blades of grass. She walked to the center of the field. Tarma wouldn't be able to resist the bait.

A screech sounded behind her, just before a shadow blocked the moon, casting the field into momentary darkness. Ashley crouched as Tarma dove. Ashley spun and caught Tarma's leg. The beast lurched, off balance now that the slash that had been meant for Ashley's chest raked her arm instead.

Tarma's wings tangled under her. Ashley didn't hesitate to leap upon the sprawled demon. As Ashley moved, her form changed. The form that had so controlled her at the motel rose to the surface, though instead of fearing the demon, now she embraced it. Claws bit into Tarma's scales as Ashley swiped at her foe. The slim yet powerful tail balanced her as she reared back to deliver another blow. Teeth gnashed as Ashley struck again and again.

The warm flow of Tarma's blood trickled down and around the disturbed scales. The beast fought for breath.

Ashley stood and relaxed into her own form. Her arm burned. The light blue blouse she wore now hung like ticker tape from her shoulders. Only the collar held the fabric on her frame. Blood had stained her bra and the scraps of her shirt. The demon within her was braced just under the surface.

Tarma grunted and hissed as she rolled and clawed to her feet. Her tail no longer swung but rested limply on the ground behind her. Still, Tarma grinned when she saw Ashley the woman standing in front of her. Tarma's fangs clacked as she spoke. "Do you think you can get away with murder? Lena was your sister."

"So was Nichole." Ashley thought of the innocent girl several times a day. "And how many other sisters did you kill because they refused to follow blindly in feeding the souls of men to demons?"

"Only the Mother can make the call to retire a sister. You are not in the inner circle yet." She chuckled the dry, raspy sound of sandpaper. "You judge the demon, but you've accepted it well enough. Your bond is almost complete."

The thought chilled Ashley's blood. She would not be a demon's puppet. "I want out of the sisterhood entirely."

"It's too late. You're more a part of us now than you ever were. You will be punished for Lena, but you will learn." Tarma shifted her head toward the house, as if listening. "The Mother decides who goes and on what terms."

A door shut. Ashley could hear Ryan sprint across the gravel driveway and into the clearing.

"You think playing house with these werewolves will protect you from your destiny?" Tarma growled. "It's already inside you."

Ryan slowed and leveled his gun at Tarma's massive frame. Even injured, Tarma could rip him to bits, so Ashley moved between them. Tarma would have to go through her to hurt her new family.

Another raspy laugh. "You may end me, but the Mother can reach you here. She can reach you anywhere. Your new pets will never be safe."

"They will not be harmed."

"Once your transformation is complete, the Mother need only reach our her hand to control you. You will kill them all yourself. You have no choice." Tarma crept to her right, and Ashley matched her steps.

"There's only one alternative." Ashley felt the beast rise within her again. "You all must die." Wings spread. Claws sprouted from her fingertips. She would end this threat now.

A baby's wail pierced the air.

Ashley stopped and glanced back.

Ryan straightened and did the same.

"Ah. Another pet," Tarma purred. "You could swallow that one whole, you know, and if it's male, it would be the sweetest treat you could imagine."

Ashley rounded, and Ryan advanced, both growling.

Tarma launched herself and wobbled in the air a moment. "You have till sunrise. Deliver yourself or the Mother will have you dispatch your pets and return. You will come back to us, all the same." A powerful beat of her wings and Tarma lifted further into the air. She circled the house screaming before flying into the night.

"Are you all right?" Ryan closed the distance, ignoring Ashley's wings and still whipping tail.

She didn't need to debate this. Changing into her own form would mean discussion. Discussion would mean at least Eric coming along, and she couldn't put him in danger. As it was, she'd already interfered in Ryan and Lydia's happy world. She wouldn't cause anyone else misery.

"Tell Eric I'll be back by dawn." The cries of the newborn quieted. Eric would be out soon. If she saw him she'd never be able to leave. "Go. Take care of that baby."

She leapt into the air; perhaps this was the one thing she'd miss once she returned the ring, provided she was able to survive the night.

Ryan shouted something unintelligible as her powerful wings lifted her into the sky and away from her love. For years, she'd given the concept of love no thought. Then, for one brief moment, she'd permitted herself to dream of a family, a future. She had to protect everything she held dear, the prospect of raising children with a man who completed her more than the sisterhood ever had. Eric would understand. He had to.

Cities scrolled beneath her as she winged her way back to Las Vegas.

• • •

"It's a girl," Eric quietly announced as Ryan approached his sleeping wife and child.

Ryan stroked his wife's hair, then stood, and took Eric's shoulder. "Ashley said to tell you she would be back by dawn."

"Back by dawn? Where the hell did she go?" Eric struggled to keep his voice hushed, though even as he asked, he knew the answer.

Ryan's hand reached as if aching to caress the child's head. "The demon told her if she didn't they would kill us all." He met Eric's gaze. "She didn't give me a chance to talk her out of it. She said she'd be back," Ryan repeated.

The urge to race out the door was so strong, but Eric sat. Slowly. "No, she won't. She's trading her life for ours."

Ryan unfolded the baby quilt Eric's nana had given them and tucked in his wife and child. "Go after her."

Eric stood. Then sat, rubbing a hand through his hair. "They flew. I'll never make it in time."

"Call Silas." Lydia opened an eye just a bit. "Remind him of that article you wrote a few years back. He kept saying he owed you because his business went through the roof."

Ryan had his cell out and was already dialing. "I interviewed him for an article about the market for small plane tours. He cashed in on the publicity and has called me several times to offer us trips here and there. I'll tell him this makes us even, and maybe he'll leave it alone." He smiled at his wife. "Two birds, one stone."

"Glad I could help," Lydia muttered as she closed her eyes again.

•••

To avoid being seen Ashley attempted to fly over the less inhabited areas. She hugged treetops to stay off the radar. When she reached the desert she flew as low as she could, though the sand still radiated around her head and the thermal seemed to want to lift her higher into the air.

Perhaps by the end of the day she'd be worthy of Eric. He fought his fears daily. He had the most beautiful aura.

He said they were mated, and though she hadn't known him to lie, it was hard to believe so simple a thing as sex could irrevocably bind them. It had been years, but she remembered what great sex was, and it *was* great sex. Was it more? Maybe. Probably. Toward the end, before all the nerves in her body ignited, there might have been something. She'd felt closer to him than everyone. Even now, she seemed to feel his heart breaking. Or maybe it was hers.

The lights of Vegas lit the horizon. She couldn't simply fly up to the sisterhood's house. She'd have to land on the outskirts and probably borrow a car. If she lived, she'd return it; if not, the sisters would move it to a place where it would be safe till found. They'd had to borrow vehicles in the past. They'd always seemed to do the right thing, like returning them.

Things like that were what had kept her so blind for so long. She'd saved all those women from toxic relationships, and she'd been stuck for years in the worst one of all.

• • •

Silas landed his small four-seater plane on the closest airfield to the succubus mansion. "Sorry I can't take you closer."

"Don't worry about it." Eric climbed down and began to sprint across the pavement.

Silas called after him, "Do you want me to stay a day or so … in case you can't find your girl? Vegas is a big city."

"Thanks, but I have a very good idea where I'll find her."

Chapter 15

Night still covered the sky, though the stars seemed to disappear in the east. Only about two hours till sunrise. The sisters would be readying themselves for her arrival. Of course she would come.

Ashley prayed, to any deity listening, that somehow their attention would be drawn elsewhere so she could acquire the element of surprise, but of course she knew better.

She landed in a small park at the edge of the housing complex. Few were out and about this time of day. Mostly joggers in spandex with their earbuds in, eyes focused on the road ahead and minds engaged in their own worlds. She descended in a small stand of juniper.

She would require a disguise, as she couldn't wander around Vegas as a demon. She assumed the appearance of someone on their morning run.

She jogged in place a moment or two before emerging from the brush, and trotted toward the path. Her lungs filled with the fresh morning air, the rhythm of her shoes on the pavement reminded her of the beat of her wings. In another life, she could really have enjoyed the run. But today—

A huge black figure bolted from across the deserted playground. It headed straight for her.

She braced herself, ready to shift. Then she got a good look at the creature and saw herself in his heart. She ran to meet him, cursing. "Stupid" and "pigheaded" were the nicest things she said.

In a bound, he shifted into himself, naked as a jaybird. His self-satisfied smirk was the only thing stopping her from smacking him.

"I told you not to follow me." She was barely able to rein in the shout.

He slipped a backpack from his shoulder and unzipped it. "No, you didn't."

"I told Ryan to tell you."

"You told Ryan to say you'd be back in the morning." He dressed as if they were in private. Then he stopped, barefoot and bare-chested, to catch her hand. "It's morning, and I'm an impatient man. You can't expect me to wait until the sun is up to see you."

She growled. "I wanted you to be safe. This isn't your fight. This isn't their fight. You all are my family now. Just being around me puts you in danger. But I can fix that."

He pulled on an old Van Halen t-shirt and sat on a nearby bench for his socks and sneakers. "Couples compromise. I left the rest of the family at home." Dressed, he pulled two guns and four clips from the backpack and tossed the empty sack under the bench. "We didn't all come. Ryan is following your instructions to look after his baby. They both send their regards, by the way."

She swatted at him. He easily ducked and then caught both of her arms. "When I was human, I thought I would fall in love and get trapped in marriage by some woman eventually. When I became … this, I was broken. I couldn't even date anymore. I thought there was no hope of finding anyone that would be able to deal with the monster that I've become." She started to protest, but he lifted a finger and continued. "Then, there you were. Accepting me for everything I am and reminding me that even as this"—he tapped his chest—"I can do so much good. I will not lose, you know." He ran a finger under her jawline. "I'm much too stupid and pigheaded for that."

They crossed the lawn and stood before the ornate door. It had never been locked before, and today was no different. She placed a hand on the latch and pushed. It swung open without a sound. They both hesitated.

"Is anybody home?" Eric whispered. "We'd like to kill you now."

She elbowed him and received a wink in return. He'd given her one of his guns and an extra clip. They raised their weapons now as they crossed the threshold. Nothing. No sound other than their breathing.

When she turned around he was admiring the mural. "I'm no art critic, but this is kind of nice."

She rolled her eyes and glanced in the adjoining rooms. No sign of anyone. She crossed to the entrance to the kitchen. Nothing. She expected someone to be around. They knew she was coming. Someone should have been there to greet her. Or at least take her into custody.

Then she heard it, and her shoulders tightened. Chanting came from the door under the stairs. The basement. They'd started a ritual. One she didn't recognize.

Her blood ran cold, and for the twentieth time, she mentally cursed that Eric had tagged along.

She gripped his arm. "I don't want you going down there. They will tear you to pieces just because you're a man."

The corner of his mouth twitched. He placed a hand on the doorknob. "Shall we?"

She kissed him and then nodded. They were outnumbered, and the Mother had more magic in one pinky than Ashley had ever dreamed of having. She was with Eric, they were together; hopefully that was all they needed.

She descended the stairs first. Every step was familiar. She ran her hand along the wall; her fingertips recognized every cool stone. This place had been her home for decades. She'd laughed and cried in this house alongside these women. The sisterhood had been her family. Now, without hearing her out, they'd turned on her and would destroy her new family. The people who truly loved her.

But the sisterhood loves you. We would give all to see you succeed. You belong with us.

Her body trembled. *This man hasn't given anything. He's stolen your heart, tampered with your mind. He doesn't deserve to hold your soul.* Ashley's stomach soured. *You should take it back. Take back your soul. Rip it out. Rip it out.*

She stopped and braced her hands on either wall.

Rip it out. Take it back.

No, he hadn't stolen anything. She'd given it to him.

Rip it out. Take it back.

She'd welcomed him. She loved him. She swayed under the pressure.

• • •

Eric stopped behind her. He couldn't understand the chant, but he did feel its weight. It pushed on his body like the pressure of a plane at takeoff. The sisterhood knew they had entered the mansion. They pressed into the couple's minds.

Ashley had braced herself in the passageway, her head bowed. He knew she felt the chanting more than he did. He wanted to help her. But how? He reached out a hand and laid it on her back. "I love you," he whispered.

She gasped. Her whole body went rigid. Then, after a few moments, she turned her pale face to him. "Thank you," she whispered.

He didn't know what he'd done, or how it worked, but he sent out a silent prayer of thanks that it had.

The chanting continued to get louder the deeper they went. Finally, he couldn't take it anymore and called out, "Your nasty singing won't stop us. We will end you."

Eric's voice echoed through the stairwell, and the chanting faltered.

Then Ashley herself giggled, and the tinkle of it reverberated against the stone, again tripping up the chanting.

She called out to the chanting women. "The sisterhood is run by demons. The Mother and Tarma are not what you think. We don't have to kill the men. They can be saved. We can make a difference without demons. Come with me. Let me show you how."

She reached back and took his hand, and together they descended the stairs to the bottom. The chanting continued, but the damage was done. The pressure was alleviated. The passage curved at the bottom, but before they turned the corner and faced the hordes that wanted to kill them he needed to do one thing.

He reached for Ashley and kissed her deeply. They were joined. They were one. Male and female. They had balance. When she leaned back, she said, "I love you."

She passed him her gun. He started to try to stop her. But she raised a finger to her lips, stepped back, faced the chanting, pulled a knife from her pocket, and made to cut off the finger with the black onyx ring. Around the corner, the room erupted in screams, halting her knife and causing it to fall from her fingers. Running footsteps warned them of their approach. Eric passed Ashley back her gun and stepped to her side.

Seconds later, several women sprinted around the corner. And Eric opened fire. In such a narrow hall the noise set their ears ringing instantly. It was easy for him to pick them off. With strangled cries, they fell to the floor.

They came in waves. One group would fall, a few moments would pass, and another would round the bend.

• • •

Ashley stood rooted to the spot, gun half raised, holding back sobs. Nine had fallen. They came without weapons. Nothing but their raised hands and hollow screams to defend themselves. There was only one word for it. Slaughter.

"Stop," Ashley called to the Mother creature who held sway over these women. "You're killing them. Give them a choice. Let them flee."

"They had their choice. They are part of the sisterhood. They've been freed from the influence of those like the murderer beside you. Did you think they would not die for this freedom, for the power you would so easily cast aside?"

Running steps heralded their approach. Eric raised his weapon and looked at Ashley. He would lower his weapon if she asked. She shook her head. He lowered his gun.

With a deep breath, Ashley raised her own and eliminated the last three. Jessie. Meredith. Lacey. The last of her sisters fell. They weren't innocent. They'd ripped out and devoured hundreds of men's souls. But, like her, they'd been duped. They had been sold on the corruptness of men by a master of manipulation and corruption. There was no way to save them. No way to explain how they'd been misguided. To give them the gift she'd been given. She lowered her gun. When this was over she'd mourn the lives they could have had.

But it wasn't over yet. Eric took Ashley's hand and led her over the bodies of the crumpled women.

Through the arched doorway, they could see an altar flanked by two demons. Although she'd been in this room before, all the comfort and belonging she'd known here was gone.

The smaller of the two hissed. Tarma obviously hadn't been able to return to human form. Scales were missing. Her wounds still oozed. She couldn't heal. Still, she limped toward them. "You've made a mistake, sister." For some reason, they still wanted to turn her back.

"I've made my choice." Ashley's voice echoed through the cavern. "You can still be saved." Ashley knew in her heart that

Tarma would never leave the Mother's side, but if there was a slim chance that her friend and mentor could be freed she had to try.

"You're forsaking a great gift," Tarma grumbled and hobbled around to their left, causing them to sidestep closer to the Mother.

The Mother approached the pair, her arms outstretched. "You've fallen for this man. We can forgive that. You should concentrate on your other new relationship."

As she spoke, Ashley felt her skin writhe and the slits for her scales open. Instead of becoming the beast, she felt its presence inside her. This was a new kind of shifting. The demon meant to completely take her over.

"It's a love more complete than you'll ever know. A love no human can give or understand."

Where the pieces of Eric's soul were warm and filled with light, the demon was a void. Not warm. Not cold. Nothing. And it was spreading. The ring burned; the darkness spread.

"No," Ashley commanded. "I am done with the sisterhood. I will not be a demon's puppet." She pushed as hard as she could against the darkness. She felt Eric's love and concentrated on how much she loved him back, on the possibilities, on their bright future, and the glow brightened. It warmed. As the rest of her lit up like a glow stick, the ring faded and faded. Finally, with joy, she slipped it off of her finger.

Tarma's tail got a little more life in it as she directed her muzzle toward Eric. "I've been given the honor of killing you myself, *dog*. I'll enjoy every minute." She crossed the distance between them in two steps.

Claws extended, she shoved Ashley aside and lunged at Eric.

• • •

He raised his weapon when the first demon started moving. When claws and fangs charged him, instinct had him unloading his clip into the dripping maw. But it kept coming. He felt its claws on his arms.

"The first thing I will remove is your balls, you pitiful creature." It punctuated its statement by digging its claws into his thighs. Points of fire arched his back and had him screaming in agony.

He heard a deep chuckle, and the pain receded. Eric opened his eyes to a sheet of rock. The demon held him to the ceiling. "No!" He heard Ashley scream.

"I will be doing you a favor, sister. That part just causes trouble anyway."

His gun had fallen from his hands. He tried to shift to the wolf, only to realize he already had. His claws scraped impotently against the demon's scales. He twisted in the grip to see Tarma's maw open. The scent of decay wafted from the demon's throat. Even as the teeth neared, he could see Ashley scrabbling on the ground for the ring she'd tossed.

"No," was the only thought he could muster as his head disappeared into the dark.

An impact brought him back into the light. Another sent him flying through the air. Inhuman screams echoed in the chamber. The strike of the floor on the back of his head plunged him into darkness.

• • •

Ashley gave herself over to the beast and spared Tarma no mercy. She barely noticed as Eric flew across the room. She gripped Tarma's throat in her mouth and bit. Scales popped and flesh wrenched.

The human part of herself cheered as the demon within her belched forth fire and roasted the mangled husk of what used to be Tarma. She reveled in the flames. Even after her foe was nothing but a charred lump of nothing on the floor, she kept the flame on.

You've made the right choice, the Mother cackled in her mind. *Now, the mongrel.*

Ashley turned. Eric's bloody body lay in a heap on the floor.

The demon within her bubbled flames to the surface. *Roast the mongrel.*

No. Ashley struggled to regain control. The demon pressed. Ashley twisted. The demon turned. She had no control anymore. The wings, the teeth, the fire all belonged to the demon.

Except for a finger. One finger on her right hand. She concentrated all of her energy. The finger moved, taking the unsuspecting arm with it. She curled the finger around the ring and pulled. The demon realized too late what she'd done. The dark band fell to the ground. In a scream chorused by the Mother, Ashley regained control.

She ran to Eric, not raising her head when the Mother roared again.

"Eric. Oh, Eric," Ashley cried. Blood poured out of everywhere. She tore at her clothes to make bandages to stop the bleeding. She pressed frantically on the wounds on his chest.

Ignoring the Mother as she moved to scoop Tarma off the floor, Ashley focused everything she had on Eric. *You can heal. You can do this.*

Finally, his eyes fluttered open, and he groaned.

"Oh, thank God," Ashley whispered, gathering him close.

The Mother roared.

Ashley stood, placing herself between the Mother she'd come to loathe and the man she'd never believed she could love.

"I will drink his soul and yours with it." The Mother once again came out from behind the altar. "I will have you both."

No! The word didn't scream from her lips, but broadcast from her heart. Like a supernova, the power of their combined souls ripped from her chest. The last thing Ashley saw as her life flowed from her was the Mother reduced to ashes.

Chapter 16

Two women were sitting on a rock at the edge of a babbling brook, their bare feet swinging to sweep toes into the warm water. "Is this heaven?" Ashley asked.

Nichole laughed. "What if it is?"

"I don't deserve heaven."

"Oh, but you do. You gave your life for your love, for your family. Self-sacrifice is the sign of a noble heart. Don't you realize how much you have changed? I've learned that everyone gets a second chance, every day. It's how you choose to use those chances that makes you good or evil."

"I'm dead. Out of chances."

Nichole arched an eyebrow. "Do you remember the mural on the mansion wall?"

As if in answer to Nichole's question, they were buffeted by rhythmic gusts of wind. From the sky descended what looked like a white dragon.

"We've got a proposition for you."

• • •

Eric was alone. The room echoed every breath, every pant, as he pulled himself toward where Ashley lay in a pile of ashes, her body charred, a gaping hole in her chest.

"No." His back and chest ached. "Ashley." He had to get to her. The couple of feet he had to go felt like a mile.

The air stank of sulfur and burnt hair. Ashes tickled his nose and made his eyes water. He had to get to her. She couldn't be … She just couldn't be …

"Ashley." He choked out her name again. "Ashley." He reached for the fabric of her blouse. His fingertips brushed her arm. Another shove with his toes and he gripped her forearm.

No. She was already going cold. Tears fell unchecked from his face. He managed to push himself up and turn her head to face him.

He heard footsteps on the stairs. "Help," he called, cradling her head in his arms. "Please help her."

The steps ran now.

Aaron and several police officers rushed into the basement, guns drawn. When he saw Eric on the ground he ran over. "No." Aaron ordered the officers upstairs to retrieve the EMTs.

Aaron pressed his fingers to Ashley's throat and, after a minute, shook his head.

A note rang through the room, echoing like the chanting. Though, where the other pressed, this freed. The sound reverberated and grew in harmony and complexity. Aaron crouched next to Eric, his face twisted in confusion.

Then, something happened. Did she move? "Ashley?" Eric whispered her name as if to gently wake her.

And she breathed in, sucking in air as if rising from the water. Her eyelids fluttered and opened. She managed a weak smile and took his hand in hers. Another ring adorned her finger, this one opal. The lights within it seemed to continue the music as the sound faded.

Eric brushed his bruised lips over Ashley's. It was over.

Aaron cleared his throat. "I don't mean to interrupt, but there were reports of gunfire." He stood and surveyed the room. "There are no bodies, but I'm going to have to explain this." He paused and looked at the couple. "Those gangs are getting out of control."

Ashley and Eric rose to their feet.

"You all need a ride anywhere?" Aaron asked.

"No." Ashley smiled. "We're going to fly home, but I have one thing to do first."

Chapter 17

Ashley walked into the hospital disguised as a petite brunette with a pixie haircut. She wore scrubs and a name tag that she shifted to match those that the other nurses wore.

She entered with a throng of other nurses on their way in to work. Nobody paid attention to the new nurse. She knew exactly where she was going.

Finally, she saw the faint glow of the tiny piece of Nichole's soul. It was faint; it had entered a hostile environment and seemed about to lose the fight.

She walked into the room, quickly shutting the door behind her. She could see his body.

She walked past the empty bed nearest the door and lifted the chart on the second. Though the man still repulsed and infuriated her, this was her first act as a vessel of light. She was determined to do right by him, so she refused to look at the man in the bed. She read the name. William.

Naming him made it easier to see him as a person. With a deep breath, she reached out and touched his mind. She could see him as a boy, spoiled rotten by rich parents. As a young man on the fast track to success, dancing a jig on the backs of the little people, because it was what everyone expected.

And when the time came to have a wife and family, they needed to fit the mold he'd worked so hard to achieve. But they only disappointed him, because unlike his dreams, they were imperfect and that was unacceptable.

The man in the bed before her was broken, but not beyond repair. She only hoped that she would be able to do the job and return him to his wife. It was the least the poor woman deserved.

Ashley replaced the chart and looked at the man, at William. The wisps of graying strawberry-blond hair framed his head on the pillow. His pale face was drawn and relaxed.

In her years with the sisterhood she'd stripped a man's soul bare by inciting fear, but she'd never tried to heal someone. Her new power told her where to start, so she swallowed her new instinct and touched her hand to his forehead.

Fear. She could feel it radiating from him. She knew she remained the object of his fear. Hopefully, she could help him become a better person. The one time she'd cleansed a soul before, she hadn't meant to do it. She hoped the ability would not elude her. Over and over again, she reached into his soul and removed the evil bits. Finally, after what seemed like hours, she was done.

His vitals remained the same. The evil was gone, but he couldn't seem to wake up.

She reached her consciousness into his chaotic flow of thought. Scenes floated about her like movie screens playing scenes of his life. Every memory played on the screens. Then she saw the block, the fear that stopped him from regaining consciousness.

Standing, floating in the center of a long hall appeared to be Nichole, or at least the form Nichole took when she lured him. At her feet, what appeared to be a little boy cowered.

"Why are you here?" Ashley asked the apparition, but it didn't respond.

As Ashley approached the shuddering boy, William as a youth, he whimpered and shook, muttering something that sounded like a prayer.

Ashley looked again at the image hovering over them; though it still seemed to be Nichole she could see many differences.

The most obvious was a long, thin branch in her hand. A switch.

"You've been a bad boy." The image grinned and ran a hand down the length of the switch. "Now Nanny needs to punish you."

The boy's nanny closely resembled Nichole. That explained a lot. Little William was given everything with one hand and then was neglected and beaten with the other.

"I told you not to gulp so loudly. I don't like to hear you chew," the nanny exclaimed.

"I'm sorry, I'm sorry," the child sobbed.

Ashley moved between the child and nanny. "You will not beat him anymore."

The figure of the nanny screamed, dropping the stick and tearing at her hair.

"He is a good boy and can be a good man if you stop beating him." This woman must've been why he hated women. Ignored by his mother and beaten by his nanny.

Ashley turned to the little boy and, laying her hands gently on his head, let the healing power run through her and into the boy's mind. "Not all women want to hurt you, William. Your wife loves you and just wants to be loved in return."

Behind them, she could hear the nanny groaning. As she healed the boy, it destroyed the apparition that so horrified him.

So she concentrated harder. "You are a good boy. A good man."

"No, he's mine. Nooo," the figure wailed then screamed.

Ashley stroked the boy's hair. "I'm so proud of you, William," she said, keeping her tone gentle but speaking loud enough that he could hear over the nanny's screams.

Finally, the screaming stopped. Ashley spared a glance over her shoulder and saw nothing. The hall behind them was empty.

When she turned back to the boy he smiled up at her.

"Thank you."

"You're very welcome." She smiled back.

They both stood and walked down the hallway.

Ashley faded back to herself. How long she'd actually stood by the bed she couldn't tell, but her legs ached a little when she stepped back.

William's eyes opened. "Oh." He shifted and, realizing he was hooked up to equipment, his expression changed to bewilderment. "What am I doing here? Was I in an accident?"

"Um." She wasn't prepared to answer questions. A couple of voices could be heard outside the door.

"Are you sure you want to remove him from life support, ma'am?"

"He wouldn't want to live this way."

"Marie?" William croaked when he tried to call out.

"Bill?" Marie ran around the divider curtain to the bed. "He's awake." She touched his face. He was smiling at her.

"I thought you'd left me." Marie's tears ran down her face.

He placed his hand over hers. "I love you, darling."

The doctor looked at Ashley. "When did he awaken?"

"Just now, Doctor," Ashley replied. When the doctor picked up the chart, Ashley edged around the curtain and slipped out of the door.

• • •

Ashley had once wondered how many chances someone gets to remake their life.

They pulled up in front of Eric's grandmother's house. The idea of meeting the most important woman in his life scared her slightly. "Are you going to tell her anything about being a werewolf? Or about what I've become?" Ashley asked as they ascended the front stairs.

"Never is soon enough," he said as he opened the screen door at the same time Nana opened the heavy door.

They hugged in greeting. Once inside, Eric said, "Nana, I'd like to introduce you to my wife, Ashley."

Instead of anger, Nana laughed and hugged her.

Pleased, Eric said, "I'm going to go open this wine."

Nana took Ashley's hands. "Welcome to the family, dear." She linked elbows with Ashley and led her inside.

Nichole's voice whispered in Ashley's ear, "To answer your question, you have endless chances. Every instant you live is an opportunity for another choice toward happiness."

After six months, she'd have that murdering bastard locked down. In less than two hours things would be in place. She just had to handle one thing first.

"Alan, this isn't a good time." She moved the cell phone to her other ear and pulled her holster and weapon out of her desk drawer. Why did men always get clingy after three dates?

"It's never a good time for you, Lydia." Even over the phone she could see his disapproving scowl.

Struggling not to simply hang up, she pushed the button to switch the phone to speaker and sat it on her desk. "In case you forgot, I'm a cop; on call for stakeouts and killer catching."

The phone stayed silent as she strapped on her vest and settled her holster. Did he hang up? "Alan?"

"I had a night planned." His voice trembled. *Oh God, was he going to cry?* "It's our one-month anniversary."

She shifted her vest and stared at the phone. It should be a romantic gesture. Most women would love a guy who plans a special night. But all she could focus on was how the whine in his voice so closely matched nails on a chalkboard.

"Detective Davis?" Sergeant Eric Adams leaned into her office. "Ready?"

"Who is that?" Alan yelled. The tremor in his voice had turned hard. The scowl was back and something more. Something she wanted no part of. "Are you blowing me off for someone else on our anniversary?"

Lydia pinched the bridge of her nose and retrieved her cell from her desk, switching off the speaker as she did. She was about to lead a team of officers on a sting to catch a serial killer. The culmination of months of work. She didn't want to waste energy on this.

Adams cringed, but didn't appear at all contrite. She flipped him off then faced away from the door.

"Alan," she said, using the tone she reserved for frightened children. "You're right, this isn't fair to you. Go. Have a great life. I wish you all the best in the world."

"Wait — " She closed the phone on whatever would come next. Meaningless drivel or manly tirade, it would only make her late. Sometimes simply hanging up was best.

She tossed the phone on her desk and crossed the bullpen with Adams at her heels.

"Ready?" he asked.

"I've been ready to catch this guy for months."

• • •

"Is he in there?" Detective Lydia Davis asked as she approached the officers on scene.

She already had one officer down tonight. She couldn't let the bastard get away again.

"Yeah, we have two guys watching the rear," Sergeant Adams answered. "He hasn't come out yet."

The bastard was cornered now. She paused in front of a Cape Cod located in a quiet suburban neighborhood. It didn't fit the profile. Of course, this nut didn't fit any profile. Her men had pulled halfway into the driveway, blocking in an old brown station wagon. Maybe the killer's car? The smell of freshly cut grass filled her nostrils as she stood behind the SUV. Ah, the suburbs.

"Good." She didn't take her eyes off the house. "Could he have hostages in there?" she asked, anxious at the prospect of adding more casualties to the operation.

"No one went in with him. It's been for sale by owner for the last month and vacant."

"We can't wait for the rest of the team. Surprise is our best option." She took a breath, saying a silent prayer that she made the right choice. "Adams and you three, with me. The rest of you circle around and enter through the back of the house. Everyone be careful. This man is a savage."

She readied her weapon and moved past the station wagon to press against the yellow vinyl siding of the house. She and her team took positions in the flowerbeds lining either side of the door and waited several moments to allow the others to get into position.

After a silent count, she nodded to Adams and moved to open the door. Reaching for the knob, the loud report of a shotgun sounded from around back, echoing off surrounding houses, followed by measured shots from officers.

He was armed. *Not good.* But being under fire should distract him from the front and give her team the time they needed to enter. With adrenaline pumping, she fought to keep tight control of her emotions as she flung the door open and ran through, following closely behind Adams.

They entered into a front room left bare except for blinds and curtains over the front picture window. Motioning the other three to check the rest of the house, she and Adams moved through the room to the archway on their right.

This room was also completely empty. Not even dust gathered in the corners. In this room, however, the sweet smell of rotted meat filled her nostrils. She'd smelled worse, but it didn't bode well. She discovered another door to her left. This one appeared able to swing both ways.

The shotgun blasts were coming from behind that door. Lydia and Adams set up to enter. She motioned to Adams that she was going to look first. Bracing in anticipation of the horrors she may witness, she pushed the door open a crack. The smell of urine and ammonia burned her nose as she peered inside for an instant.

A beaker with tubes attached over a burner sat on a table in the corner. Boxes of sinus medicine and rat poison were stacked on the floor against the wall. Bags of what could only be crystal meth lay piled on the counter next to a set of old-fashioned scales.

Scanning, she caught sight of the killer. A very large man, about six foot two, stood in profile and glanced out the window of the back door, shotgun at the ready. Two inches of spotty growth covered his chin. His matted and greasy hair hung limp around his ears. Sweat and blood stained his clothes.

Then the man froze, ceasing his ragged growling gasps. His long nose sniffed the air as he turned. Barring his teeth in a vicious sneer, he swung the shotgun around and fired, blasting a plate-sized hole in the door.

As the door swung back from the blast, Lydia dropped to a knee, kept the door wedged open a second, and fired two rounds before spinning away. Both shots took the killer in the chest.

A scream that sounded more like a howl came from the murderer as he fired twice more. One shot took out the bottom corner of the door. The other exploded through the doorjamb inches from her elbow.

Adams caught the door on its swing and held it open for Lydia to take aim. Ferocious gunfire came through the back door. Again, she peered into the kitchen to see if the killer was down.

Pushed against the kitchen table by the gunfire coming through the rear entrance, the killer growled. His abdomen appeared riddled with wounds and blood streamed onto the floor, yet he still stood with his gun up and returned fire.

"Watch the beakers!" She yelled the precaution as she aimed for the man's head. One wrong move and they'd go up in flames.

The murderer turned at the sound of her voice. His ice-blue eyes locked with hers, and he grinned as she fired twice into his head.

The look in his eyes made her blood run cold. Even as his head rocked back, he let out a blood-curdling howl, but he just wouldn't go down. *God, how is he still moving?* He let the shotgun fall from his hands as he stepped toward her. His stare burned with a pleasure too focused to be drug-induced.

Again she fired, putting two more rounds into his skull. He fell on the table, hitting the lab. Flames exploded over the wall, spreading quickly. *Damn.*

"Get out of here!" Lydia ordered. Her officers moved out of the house, away from the flames and rolling black smoke. She glanced over her shoulder at the man she had tracked for months. Flames licked at his clothes as he lay in the wreckage. She'd wanted to bring him to justice, but that wasn't an option now.

You will be judged by a higher power today, she thought, as she exited amid a cloud of smoke.

The fire trucks had arrived. Lydia ran to the fire chief and reached out her hand. "You should know there was a meth lab inside and the body of our perp is in the kitchen."

The chief nodded and turned to do his job. She turned to her men, now gathered around their cars, waiting for her orders. The massive fire raging behind her illuminated their soot–covered faces.

It had been a long night. A quick head count told her she hadn't lost anyone else. Her men were proud, and the pleasure at taking this criminal off the streets was infectious.

She smiled. "Good work, guys."

"You got him, Davis," said Sergeant Adams.

"*We* got him," she corrected.

The other officers mirrored their grins, white teeth and eyes bright in the dimness of the evening, despite their fatigue. Their zeal improved her already good mood.

"Yup, no matter how hopped up he was, no way he walked out of there with a bullet in his head and covered in flames." She turned to look at the fire. It still raged, but the fire crews had it under control.

People crowded the nearby yards to view the spectacle. "Everyone loves to watch a fire," she muttered. She shook her head and ordered everyone to the precinct. With the exciting stuff over, they had paperwork to start. They grumbled as they headed for their vehicles. She chuckled and moved to her SUV.

"Lieutenant, can you make a statement?"

Lydia's shoulders slumped. Ryan Williams, a reporter for the *Daily Times*. Covering the murders, he'd dogged her every move for the last six months. She suspected he listened to his police scanner like most people listened to the normal radio.

She turned and looked up into a pair of magnificent green eyes. He stood several inches taller than her. He had long brown hair pulled into a loose ponytail and a closely trimmed beard, which made him look more like a biker than a prominent reporter.

A roguish smile played across his lips. "Were you able to apprehend the Bestial Butcher?"

She rolled her eyes. "Why do you insist on giving these whackos names? All it serves to do is raise them to the status of rock stars. It gives poor, twisted kids an avenue to stardom. *Oh, I'm gonna be bigger than Jack the Ripper.*" She gave Williams an icy glare and turned away.

"Did you get him?" His voice sounded strained.

She glanced over her shoulder. "I shot him between the eyes. He collapsed and set fire to himself and the house." She waved at the inferno. "No one could live through that. We'll be holding a press conference later if you want more information." She shook her head and escaped to her car.

• • •

Shaking off the effect of Detective Davis' eyes, brown streaked with gold, Ryan caught his breath. Her straight, light brown hair pulled into a no-nonsense ponytail at the nape of her neck swung slightly as she walked away. He enjoyed watching her walk. The view was a perk of following her around. She had an athletic body that confirmed the Pilates classes he'd learned she took three times a week.

He sought the same thing she did. He wanted the Butcher as much, if not more.

When he'd read several months ago that Lydia Davis was the detective assigned to the case, he knew she could track down the killer. He had to pull several strings, almost to the snapping point, to get the assignment.

The result pleased his boss. Because of the trouble the police had tracking the Bestial Butcher, several of his stories caused the paper to sell out hours after hitting the newsstand. People wrote in to give him hints and tips about who they thought the Butcher was and where they thought he hid.

Once he began passing on this information to the police, it became easier for Lydia to allow him to observe and question. She still didn't like him "tagging along," as she called it. However, she no longer threatened to arrest him when he showed up at a scene.

In fact, one of these tips started the action tonight. As the blaze consumed the remains of the house, Ryan scratched his chin thoughtfully. He climbed into his Jeep. He needed to get in place for the press conference.

* * *

Lydia eyed the collection of reporters waiting on the steps of the police station. Cameramen set up equipment along the back of a crowd. Reporters talked among themselves while they waited for her and the police chief to appear and step up to the bouquet of microphones that would catch their every word.

Inside, Lydia closed her eyes as she took a cool drink from a water fountain. Anything to quiet her shaking stomach. She hated this part of her job. She could handle a group of officers, the chief, or a stone–cold killer, but every time she stood in front of a group of reporters, she shook like a leaf.

"Simple stage fright. Nothing to worry about. You'll get used to it," they'd told her when she first made detective.

She'd been a detective for five years, and her stomach still did acrobatics when she had to talk in front of a large crowd. Taking a deep breath, she pushed the butterflies into a tight ball. Then she stood ready to face the cameras.

The chief of police, a short, balding man with salt–and–pepper hair and mustache, stomped down the hall in her direction. Although he couldn't weigh more than 145 pounds soaking wet, Chief Fairweather waddled like a man three times his size.

An injury when he worked vice forced him to desk duty. His dedication to the force and his reputation for honesty got him elected as chief of police. He had an evident air of authority as soon as he entered a room.

As he approached Lydia, he winked. "Let's do this," he said. He was a great man.

She accompanied him through the doors, and the assembled mass of reporters quieted.

The chief stepped to the microphones. "Okay, the criminal known as the Bestial Butcher is presumed to be dead, killed in a shootout when my detective and several officers attempted to apprehend him. It also appears he was a drug dealer. As we speak, the fire department is putting out a blaze that destroyed him and the vacant house where we believe he's been living. Once the fire is completely out, we'll have forensic teams going over the area, and the coroner will remove and inspect the body."

He looked out over the reporters' heads, directly into the cameras. "Because of the dedication of the police force, another criminal is off the streets." Again, he looked at the reporters. "We will now field questions."

The reporters clamored. The chief pointed to a woman from Channel Sixteen News.

"So, how many people were victims of the Butcher?"

"So far, we can attribute twenty-four slayings to him. Once his body is in the coroner's office, DNA will be taken, and we will try to match other homicides to the Butcher."

"Can you give us some background on the killings?"

Lydia glanced at the chief, and at his nod, she responded. "At first, the laceration patterns on the victims appeared as if an animal had attacked them. In fact, after the first victim, police assumed they looked for a rabid animal." Through act of sheer will, she kept her limbs from betraying her nerves.

"Only after the body count increased did homicide get called in; the killer was human. He hunted in an area too widespread for an animal to traverse. Several victims were attacked inside their apartments. We considered it unlikely a rabid dog would manage to go up five flights of stairs to attack a single individual in a secured building."

More clamoring, then a man from CNN asked, "Is it true that all of the victims were women?"

Lydia answered, "No. In fact, there were several men. There was no discrimination in affluence, race, or sex. This, in particular, made it difficult to profile the killer."

The same man asked, "What led you to believe you could make an arrest this evening?"

"We had a tip that he might strike again. During the stakeout, he appeared and attacked an officer, who was acting as bait." Everyone started talking and Lydia raised her hand. "The officer wore protective gear and is in the county hospital with his family. He is doing fine."

A man with the *Times* asked, "From whom did you get this tip?"

The chief stepped forward. "C'mon, Dave, you know most tips are anonymous."

The conference continued with the reporters asking more questions about the victims and motives of the Butcher. The butterflies in Lydia's stomach once again took flight. She shifted uncomfortably. Surely this couldn't go on much longer. She scanned the journalists and noticed Ryan Williams. He stood at the far edge of the crowd, holding up a mini recorder. A flush warmed her face. Perhaps with the case over they could go out for drinks or dinner or —

"And have you already been assigned another case, detective?"

Still looking at Williams, Lydia startled at the question. She stammered at the reporter who spoke. "Um … My next case … " She glanced at Ryan and he winked. "Um … "

The chief gave Lydia an amused look. "The detective will be going on a well-deserved vacation."

Surprised, she somehow managed a smile and a nod.

"All right, everyone, thank you and goodnight." He lifted a hand in a wave, then touched Lydia's elbow. She followed him through the doors.

"What the hell was that?" he muttered under his breath as they walked to his office. "That was the most vacant expression I have ever seen. And I have never seen one on you." Walking three feet ahead, he missed Lydia's shrug.

"Sorry, I spaced out for a second." She entered his office. The only thing that distinguished it from hers was the sign on the desk, "Harold R. Fairweather, Chief of Police."

"Look, Davis." He motioned for her to sit as he rounded the desk and did the same. "I know you haven't slept for six months."

She rolled her eyes.

"I'm serious about the vacation. Take a couple days off. Go visit friends. Get a spot on the beach. Heck, sit around in your bathrobe and veg at the television for hours on end. I don't care. But you're not going to start a new case until you recoup."

"Chief — " she started to protest.

"I mean it. Don't argue with me. Get out. See you in three days." He picked up her case report and a pen. He made a show of reading for a bit, then looked at her. "You still here?"

Lydia smiled. "No, sir. Just left." She exited, shaking her head.

He took care of his force. Everyone commented on how talking to him was like talking to a father. She didn't remember hers, having transferred from foster home to foster home most of her life.

Shaking off emptiness, she headed to her office to grab her things. As she mulled over what to do with her newly acquired time, she smiled. First thing would be to soak in a hot bath.

"Taking a vacation?" Sergeant Adams looked up from his desk. When she gave him a quizzical look, he explained, "E–mail already went out."

"I've been ordered to take a couple of days off." She shrugged.

"Any plans?"

"I hadn't really thought much beyond getting cleaned up."

Adams laughed. "Make the most of it. Go somewhere you don't have to think too much."

Lydia chuckled as she went into her office and grabbed her tattered backpack from the corner where she'd tossed it three days ago. She'd lived out of her pack on more than one occasion.

Driving home, she wondered what she would do for her vacation. She really needed peace and quiet, somewhere outside the city. Maybe spend a couple days hiking or fishing. No neighbors thudding on the walls or sirens screaming down the street. And where the loudest sounds were birds tweeting. She smiled. Three days might be enough to unwind.

• • •

Ryan turned away as the press conference ended. He enjoyed seeing Lydia flustered. She controlled herself so well that he took great pleasure in baiting her. In his work, he'd dealt with plenty of detectives, and usually he had fun irritating them. They had a sense of importance third only to doctors and lawyers. They all took themselves so seriously. He couldn't help poking holes in their inflated egos.

Lydia proved more fun because she was beautiful when she got angry. Her eyes flashed and her cheeks flushed and … *Simply fantastic.*

At his Jeep, he paused, mulling over asking her to dinner. He wanted to grab a bite, and the way she'd reacted at the press conference made him think perhaps she would say yes.

"And then what?" he said aloud to no one as he got in and started the engine. He saw no real future for them.

How could he explain what would happen when they had their first fight? No, a working relationship was better for both of them. He turned on the radio and sang along to a rock song as he drove home.

As fate would have it, he lived across the street from Lydia's building. Well, not exactly fate. He'd moved into the furnished apartment once he found out she was the detective working the Bestial Butcher case.

Since their first meeting, he felt compelled to protect Lydia. She had no real idea what she had gotten involved in. Although he had no doubt she could deal with society's scum with dispatch, the Bestial Butcher was not society's typical scum.

Entering the apartment, he tossed his keys onto the coffee table. He walked to the refrigerator and opened a can of tomato juice. As the thick, tangy liquid flowed down his throat, his mind wandered.

Prowling night streets looking for the Butcher had led him to tracks only the Butcher could leave. Lydia would follow up on the tip he'd passed her. She had to.

He tossed the empty can in the recycle bin and plopped on the sofa. Although the apartment came furnished when he started leasing it, he wouldn't have decorated it any other way. Heavy furniture boasted solid wood and upholstery stuffed to overflowing. In the case of a very comfortable blue recliner, white filler peaked through seams on one side whenever someone sat in it.

Taupe walls gave the room a feeling of warmth. Neither the recliner nor the faded orange sofa matched the hunter green shag carpet or brick-colored curtains that covered a street–view picture window. Yet the place had a coziness about it. Aside from the perfect view into Lydia's apartment, the ambience had influenced his reason to live there.

His tastes had not always tended toward homey. He remembered a time when he preferred deco furniture and open space. Only in the past few years had his tastes changed to a cozier den-like atmosphere.

He closed his eyes and stretched. In the morning, he would go to the station and see what information he could get out of them about the condition of the Butcher's body... if they even found a body. He knew somehow that the Butcher hadn't died. Not even in that fire. And if he lived, the Butcher had escaped unseen. Even with all the firefighters surrounding the house and onlookers watching from the street. Next time, he would need to get to the scene sooner if he wanted to catch him.

Having that animal slip through his fingers again built a familiar rage. Knowing this emotion all too well, he rose from the couch and stood in the middle of the room with his arms outstretched. As he slowly bent to touch his fingers to the floor, the burning in his gut began to recede. He held the posture for another few moments and moved on to the warrior.

Long ago, he'd learned to control his anger with yoga. Of all the stress–reduction and anger–management techniques he'd tried, including medication, yoga worked the best. At times, he could not completely control the crazed anger that washed over him. During these times, he was glad he didn't own the furniture and didn't intend to regain his security deposit. He had kept all his real possessions in storage for the past three years.

His life had turned upside down then. He'd almost gone insane with pain and anger. Luckily, he regained his lucidity before destroying anything he valued. Once he placed his things in storage, he started his quest to track down the cause of his life's upheaval, which led him to the city and to Detective Lydia Davis. He moved into the lotus position with a smile on his face. She was something else.

She struck a chord in him that, up until they met, he did not realize existed. Oh, there had been women — some short relationships and, of course, a few one-night stands. However, in the past three years, women had held no interest for him.

That all changed when he first saw Lydia. Something awoke. It yearned for her in a primal way. It was much more than sexual, although he wouldn't mind spending several hot, sweaty nights with her.

Ryan rose from his position on the floor. The direction of his thoughts sapped the anger out of him, but his heart rate was way up. To get any sleep, he would have to spend twenty minutes under a cold shower. He went to the window to close the drapes, but took a moment to gaze toward her apartment.

A small light shone in her bedroom, and although she had drawn the shade, he could see her faint silhouette as she moved around the room. His breath caught in his throat at the sight of her. Then she stopped and started to undress, pulling off her shirt.

"Oh God," he whispered out loud, gripping the drapery with both hands. The shade did nothing to hide the roundness of her breasts as she turned, bent, and then lifted her arms over her head to allow the fabric of a nightshirt to slip over her body. She moved to the right and turned off the light.

Only after the room across the street darkened did Ryan start to breathe again. He let out the air with a shudder and released his grip on the drapes. It took every bit of his self-control to push aside the idea of going over there and knocking on her door. How he longed to caress that body. He shook his head, wanting to knock the image from his mind's eye. Finally, he turned in a daze and stalked to the bathroom and that cold shower.

In the mood for more Crimson Romance?
Check out *The Bride's Curse* by Glenys O'Connell at
CrimsonRomance.com.